Books by Jean Rezab

Richmond Sibling Series

Chokecherry Valley Comfort
Chokecherry Valley Joy
Chokecherry Valley Love
Chokecherry Valley Faith

Other Books

In This Place Together
The Prediction

CHOKECHERRY VALLEY JOY

JEAN REZAB

ACKNOWLEDGMENTS

Special thanks to the excellent editor, Denise Roeper of Eloquent Edits, LLC, (www.eloquentedits.com), for her great suggestions. They helped create a better book than I could have envisioned on my own.

Thank you to the book cover artist at Sunset Rose Books for an amazing cover.

Considerable thanks to my family who have encouraged me in my writing journey.

Thank you to Sally, Ruth, and Amy, terrific friends who are also great at running book ideas and cover designs past. I couldn't have finished this book without your help.

Special thanks to Gayle Larson Schuck for helping by editing and making suggestions for a stronger book. She writes her own books. www.gaylelarsonschuck.com

CHAPTER 1

Abby glanced at Mark as she packed her suitcase that sat on their bed. He lounged in the armchair on the other side of the bedroom, his dark hair tousled from running his hand through it constantly as he worked. Half the time he watched her, and half the time he looked down at the laptop he held.

"Are you sure you don't want to come with me? You can work remotely." Abby added another pair of jeans to her suitcase. She'd debated how many shorts and jeans to pack based on the forecast being in the seventies and low eighties—and on the insect population on her parents' farm in North Dakota.

"I'll fly out to Chokecherry Valley like we planned for a few days next week. I'm deep into this project and need to be free from distractions. We have to get it done this week."

She walked over to him and planted a kiss on his cheek. "I'll miss you. North Dakota is a long way from Texas."

He laughed. "The time will pass quickly. It will give you a chance to spend time with your parents before I get there."

"I know. You're always so loud while you're working on that computer." She looked around the room to see if she'd missed anything.

"Do you think you'll see Paul while you're there?" Mark closed the laptop and studied her expression.

"Maybe. He stayed at Mom and Dad's house for a few months, so I imagine they get along pretty well at this point." She wasn't sure how she would feel about seeing him again. She'd been so mad at him at Samantha and Amy's funeral.

She didn't know if she still blamed Paul, or if she was over her anger at him. Time would tell. She closed the top of the suitcase and zipped it shut. "Let's have breakfast, and then you can drive me to the airport."

She stepped over to the mirror and took one more look at her smooth, brown, shoulder-length hair. She'd applied a quick swipe of eyeliner and mascara. Good enough for the plane ride. Picking up her purse and carry-on bag, she left the bedroom.

Mark went over and lifted her packed suitcase from the bed. He followed her out of the room and down the stairs. "You didn't have to make breakfast today."

She laughed as he set the suitcase down by the front door and followed her into the kitchen. "I didn't make anything. Either you make something, or your choices are fruit, yogurt, or cereal."

"I think there might be a boiled egg or two," he said, rummaging around in the fridge.

"I'm having yogurt and a banana."

He passed her a yogurt. "What if you do run into Paul?"

She finished taking the lid off the yogurt container, and then looked up. "I don't know. Why are you so concerned?"

"I just don't want you to get upset."

"You mean like when I screamed at him at the cemetery, when they buried my twin sister and my little niece?" She heard the bitterness in her own voice and realized she had a long way to go to forgive Paul, even though he hadn't caused the car accident. She had wanted someone to blame, and Paul was the scapegoat. He wasn't even in the vehicle when the accident happened.

"Like that," Mark said pointedly. "You'll be okay. Just call me any time. You know I'm able to be interrupted most of the time. I only have to be at the office a few hours today and tomorrow."

"Thank you. You may regret that offer."

Mark got up from the table and gave her a hug. "You'll be okay. Call me if you need to. I'll be joining you in North Dakota soon. I love you."

"I love you too," she said. Maybe she should have told him about quitting her job yesterday, and all the things she had been thinking about recently, but she didn't want to deal with his reaction before she visited her parents in North Dakota. She needed the time to get her feelings sorted out. She was relieved about the job but felt guilty she hadn't told him how bad the situation had gotten at work.

Anxiety pressed against her chest as she thought about the future. She and Mark had drifted apart. She wasn't afraid they'd separate, but she did need them to connect again. At this point, she was too confused to even talk about her feelings. A week on the farm would relax her and take her out of her current thoughts enough to get some perspective.

They'd have plenty of time to discuss everything when Mark joined her in Chokecherry Valley. She knew procrastination wouldn't be a good thing. Mark would just have more reason to be upset with her.

CHAPTER 2

Abby got off the plane in Bismarck, North Dakota, not knowing who to expect to meet her. She wasn't sure if both her parents would be picking her up at the airport, or if it would just be one of them. Summer at the farm was a busy time. The forty-five-minute drive out to her parents' farm by Chokecherry Valley would add more time to the trip.

She looked forward to seeing them and spending some time relaxing out in the country. Houston had become so busy, and the job at the hospital where she worked had been extra demanding lately.

She sat down in the waiting area of the airport and checked her phone. Then she caught a glimpse of her dad's graying head. His tall stature was easy to see, although the airport traffic had thinned of people fairly quickly once they reached the waiting area. Then she saw her mother walking beside her father and rushed over to hug them.

"It's so good to see you." Abby felt a guilty twinge that she'd only been back once to see them since her sister and niece's funeral in January.

"Hi, Love," her mother said, hugging her back.

She got the same treatment from her father, and then they went to get her luggage.

"You both look great," she said.

They were looking much better than when she'd seen them in March three months earlier. Her father stood upright instead of emphasizing the slouch he'd developed since the funeral, and he had a summer tan that made his complexion look even darker than usual. Her petite mother smiled and looked more rested.

Abby had hated to leave them last time she visited, but she had to get back to her nursing job in Houston. At least she had these two weeks with them now.

"We caught a break this spring when Paul stayed with us and helped out with the calves and the spring planting." Her mother smiled at her. "He helped a lot."

"Now, Nina," her father said. "Paul grew up on a farm before he became a doctor, so of course he knew what to do. And he has helped me some over the years."

Not often, Abby wanted to say, but she held her tongue. She wasn't going to disrupt her parents' peace over her own anger at Paul. "Is he back working at the hospital now?"

"Yes," her mother said. "He's working full time and seems to be doing okay. He's met a nice young woman. Her name is Hannah."

"Isn't it a little soon for him to be dating?" She regretted the snippy tone, but it was too late to take it back. Abby felt irritation on her sister's behalf. Did Paul feel he could replace Sam so easily?

"They're taking it really slow."

"Too slow if you ask me," her father said.

"Frank!" Her mother playfully tapped him on the arm. "Not everyone proposes on the first date, like you did."

"When you know, you know." He hugged her.

Abby was pleased to see that they were doing so well, and some of the guilt of her neglect eased a little. She still needed to get back to see them more often though.

They left the airport and reached the pickup. Abby lifted her suitcase and carry-on into the back area of the extended cab and slid onto the seat.

"You could have sat in the front seat and talked to your dad while he drove." Her mother got into the passenger seat in the front.

"That's okay. I can be a back-seat driver from here and talk to you both."

Their drive to the farm was mostly on the highway and then about five miles on country roads. They didn't pass through the town of Chokecherry Valley, but the farm was only about three miles from the town. There was a grocery store, bar, community hall, St. Anne's Church, and a small café. For anything more, they would have to travel to one of the bigger towns in the surrounding area, or travel to Bismarck.

Abby figured Chokecherry Valley would have anything she needed at the little grocery store. Her parents tended to keep all the basics well stocked at their house.

When they got to the farm, her father carried her suitcase up to her room. Her parents had remodeled her room and Samantha's when they had both gotten married within a year of each other. Her room didn't feel the same as when she grew up, which was a little sad, but it helped that Samantha's room had also changed.

She and her parents didn't need constant reminders that Samantha was gone, even though the thought wasn't far from Abby's head for long, and she doubted it wasn't far from her parents' thoughts either. It was hard to think she wouldn't see her sister on this trip.

She sent a quick text to Mark that she had arrived, and everything had gone okay. She'd call him that evening before she went to sleep.

CHAPTER 3

I'm a Gifter. God has me gifting children to parents on Earth. I love doing that. I even get to go to Earth once in a while to help with a birth. My name is Samantha. My daughter is in heaven too, and she was at the hospital talking to another child at the last birth I attended. Ever since then, I see her often in heaven.

I got to attend little Chloe's birth. Her mother, Madison, lives in Chokecherry Valley, and Madison's mother knows my mother. I wonder if I'll be in Chokecherry Valley again? I never know why God sends me where he sends me. It's just that suddenly I'm attending a birth and giving out comforting vibes to the mother.

CHAPTER 4

Abby spent the rest of the afternoon unpacking and just talking with her parents. They had arrived at the farm from the airport about 4:00 p.m., and there wasn't much time to do anything else. She helped her mom prepare the evening meal of meatloaf, potatoes, green beans, and blueberry pie.

After they'd eaten, she helped her dad with the outside chores, and then they talked for a while before bed. Abby didn't tell them the real reason she'd taken two weeks to come visit in addition to seeing them. She was tired of working in Houston and thought a career change would help, but she needed the time away from Mark to get some perspective.

She was even thinking of moving out of Houston, and that would be a big change for Mark. She was ready for the change, but would he be interested in moving? She didn't know, and she needed to figure out a way to talk to him about it. Their marriage had developed a divide due to their constant work schedules, which she didn't like.

Her dad sent her off to bed at 10:00 p.m., saying she made him tired just watching her yawn. She laughed and said goodnight to her parents. Once she settled into the queen-sized bed in her old room, she lay there for hours, unable to sleep, but too uninterested to get up and retrieve one of the books from her suitcase to read. She'd called Mark, and they each ran through their uneventful day before hanging up.

Now, as she lay awake, she kept going through make-believe conversations with Mark about quitting her job. Since they were simply hypothetical conversations in her own head, she had no idea if they'd bear any resemblance to what the actual conversation would be once she started talking to Mark.

#

After only a few hours of sleep, she woke early and heard her parents already moving around getting ready for the day. Days on the farm started early. She showered, dressed, and joined her mom in the kitchen. Her dad had already gone out to start the farmwork for the day.

"What's your plan for today?" her mom asked.

"I'm going to help you with whatever you need." Abby took a grapefruit from the counter and poured herself a cup of coffee.

"I have to be in Chokecherry at ten to meet with the Community Helpers group. There are five of us meeting this morning, and we're going to be working on a drive for donations for a family who lost their home in a fire. I think we have a few other things on the agenda, but Melissa keeps track of that. She's our secretary."

"That sounds like a good idea. I'll go with you." Abby finished her grapefruit and sipped her coffee.

"Are you sure? This is your vacation, Love. Do you really want to come to this meeting?" Her mom finished wiping the counter and folded the dishcloth in half before putting it across the double sink.

"I'm sure." Abby shrugged. She sure didn't want to sit around the house wondering any longer about mythical conversations with Mark, or what she wanted to do with the rest of her life. Talking about someone else's problems would be good for her and take her mind off her own troubles.

A half hour later they were driving into town, which was only a few miles away from the farm. Abby was enjoying the peaceful nature of the drive. She had her window open enough to breathe in the fresh air, and the warm summer air streaming in the window blew her hair in her face. She smiled as she moved a piece of hair away from her eyes. Tall green grass and weeds filled the ditches, and she knew her dad would be out haying the ditches and grass fields that belonged to him.

"Does Dad have someone to help him with the haying now that Paul is back working at the hospital?" she asked.

"There's a neighbor whose son helps us. The kid's name is Jason. Actually, he's in his thirties, so maybe only a kid to me." Her mom glanced over at her and then back at the road. "I'm not sure if you remember Jason Allmen. His parents are Patricia and Gary."

"I remember them all. Jason was just a few years younger when Sam and I graduated from high school."

"Well, he's grown up now, but he's still cute. We're trying to find a nice girl for him."

"Mom, I know you and his mom, Patricia, are friends, so I don't envy Jason. When you get together with her, you two are always a force to fear. I imagine Jason will find himself married in the not-too-distant future."

"That's not all bad, is it? You and Mark are happy, aren't you? I was afraid that since you came without him that there was something going on."

Abby went from smiling to frowning in an instant. "Mom, I'm sorry you're worried. There's nothing wrong with Mark and me. We're just fine. We're here," she said.

Her mom pulled up in front of St. Anne's Church where the Community Helpers group was meeting. She stopped the car and shut it off. "Are you sure everything's okay with Mark? I don't want to get into your business, but I can listen."

"Really Mom, there's nothing wrong. I just needed to get away to think about work and some other stuff, but our marriage is okay. We can talk later. It looks like there are a few of the ladies standing outside waiting for us." She pointed at the church entrance.

"You're right. Now's not the time."

Abby reached out and put her hand on her mother's arm. "Thank you. And don't worry. I'm fine."

Her mom patted her hand. "Good. I'm here for you."

As they got out of the vehicle, Abby knew her mother would still be worrying about her. They would need to talk today, or her mother would imagine all sorts of things that weren't true.

Her mother introduced her to the Community Helpers group. Abby had met most of them before but was glad for the refresher in names. She'd been living with Mark in Houston for ten years and hadn't seen the women for a long time.

Christina had brought along her four-year-old granddaughter. Abby instantly fell in love with the cute, little, brown-haired child. Brooke was shy and peeked from behind Christina's leg once in a while as they all walked into the church. They settled into one of the classrooms in chairs at a round table set up for the occasion.

Melissa had already set a pitcher of water and paper cups in the center of the table along with plenty of pens and paper for any notes. Melissa smiled at Abby and pointed to the supplies. "Help yourself if you need anything. We keep this group low tech, but we do send out emails to update everyone as to what's going on with whatever project we happen to be working on."

"Thank you," Abby said. "You can add my email address to the group for this project. I'll be in town for a few weeks, and I'd love to help you out. I understand a family lost their home and belongings in a fire, and that's what you're working on right now. I'll do what I can."

Melissa's face lit up. "Thank you for being so helpful. I should have known that a daughter of Nina's would jump right in."

Melissa looked at the others seated around the table. "Since Abby has started us on the subject, let's say a quick prayer and begin."

The others agreed and then bowed their heads as Melissa said a prayer of gratitude and asked for the Lord's help in their endeavor.

When they finished praying, Christina handed Brooke a pen and some paper. "Would you like to draw a picture while we're talking?"

Brooke nodded happily and sat quietly drawing throughout the meeting.

"Our group agreed to find kitchen needs and clothing for the family. We've had enough donations from the local community to buy plates, bowls, cups, and glasses. We've also got enough money to buy each family member three sets of clothes and shoes. Who wants to take them shopping?" Nina asked.

Ellen raised her hand. "I'll take them shopping for clothes. They'll all fit in my SUV. We'll go to Bismarck. It's got enough variety for the whole family." She turned to Abby. "It's a family of four. There's a couple and their two kids. One is an eight-year-old girl, and one is a six-year-old boy. The couple is Renee and Thomas Meyer, and the kids are Zachary and Esme."

She turned to the rest of the group. "Once they've all got clothes, I'll take Renee shopping for the dishes."

Christina nodded. "I'll work on flyers for all of the surrounding communities to post in grocery stores, community halls, and churches. We'll ask for donations of items and money. She looked at Peggy. "Do you want to help me pass out the flyers to all the local communities."

Peggy nodded. She was a woman in her forties and appeared to be the shyest of the group.

She listened but didn't speak much. Between Nina, Melissa, Christina, Ellen, and Peggy, they had covered a lot of ground in the hour they gathered. When the meeting broke up, Nina and Abby had agreed to try to find a new home for the family to rent until they could either rebuild or decide what to do for a permanent home. Right now, the family was spending time at Renee's parents' house, but the home was too small to be a long-term solution.

On the ride back to her mother's house, the conversation remained focused on the Meyer family and their need for accommodations.

"I really can't think of anyone who has room for the family. I don't know of any places that are available to rent that are habitable." Her mother frowned. "I wish we had agreed to help Peggy with the flyers. Christina is much more aware of housing in the area. She sells her arts and crafts at flea markets and other events, so she knows more about what's available."

"Maybe we could have Christina help us. I'd love to watch Brooke. She's a sweet little girl. I'd be happy to do that, if it helps, so you and Christina can work on finding a home for the family."

"That's a good idea. I know Christina doesn't like to leave Brooke with a babysitter very often, but she'll know she can trust you."

"We've got two weeks while I'm here, so that should give you and Christina time to help the Meyer family find a place to live and make it habitable."

Nina smiled. "You'd think so, wouldn't you? I hope we can, but I don't know what community they're going to end up living in, and it would be nice if it's somewhere near to Chokecherry Valley since that's where their farmhouse was that burned down."

"We could spend tomorrow driving around if you want," Abby suggested. "I'd like to see what's been going on in the area where I grew up. I haven't really driven around for years. Mark and I just don't usually have the time when we visit from Houston. It'll give you and me a chance to catch up, and I can see what's going on in Chokecherry, and we can find a home for the Meyer family. Christina can let us know where to look tomorrow."

"That sounds good. I'll give her a call this evening. Tomorrow, you can tell me what's bothering you."

Abby laughed. Her mother was certainly direct, and she might as well tell her and get her opinion. "Sounds good."

"Now, let's go see what your dad is up to and if he needs anything. Jason will be gone by now. He's never here in the afternoon." She drove up the driveway to the farmhouse. "He's always back at his parents helping them by now."

"That makes a long day for him," Abby said.

"He's used to it. He's saving up money for school, so he's happy to get in the extra time, and your father can't get the haying done by himself. It works out well."

They got out of the car and walked up the front steps. "Isn't Jason getting old for college?"

"He decided to go last year and starts at the end of August, so yes, he's a little bit older than most students. His young sister had a baby yesterday, so the whole household dynamics are shifting. He's determined to go to school and get his degree though."

"Good for him. He's going after what he wants." Abby wished she knew what she wanted. She was glad she had the time at her parents' to decide. It was nice to be able to think at the end of the day here at her parents' house. After work at home there was Mark, and she was usually tired after her nursing shift at the hospital. She breathed a sigh of contentment.

CHAPTER 5

Madison looked down at the little bundle of baby in her arms and tears threatened. She held them back with effort. Chloe was the sweetest little baby girl. How could she give her up for adoption when the time came? She knew she only had a few more days before someone would come and snatch the baby away from her. Tears slid down her cheeks.

Her mother came into the room and immediately rushed over to hug Madison. "Honey, it's going to be all right. You will be okay."

Madison tugged a tissue from the box on the stand beside the bed and wiped her cheeks and nose. "What if they're not good to her?"

"We'll make sure that whoever adopts her is a good family."

Her mother's assurance only partly mollified her. "Nobody will love her as much as I do." She sniffed and blew her nose.

Her mother patted her on the arm and gave baby Chloe a kiss on the top of her head. "You're right, honey, but you know you can't keep her. We'll agree to an open adoption, so you can see her. If someone wants to adopt and keep it a closed adoption, we'll just refuse. You'll see. It will work out."

Madison adjusted Chloe's little pink booties and sighed. Her mother was right. She couldn't keep Chloe, as much as she wanted to. Chloe's father wanted nothing to do with her or the baby. He had given up his rights, and Madison was too young to give the baby a good home by herself. She still needed to finish high school. She couldn't expect her parents to give up their life to help her, even though they probably would. It was better for Chloe to have two loving parents.

"I know," she whispered. She would spend as much time with Chloe as she could, and if anything seemed off about the couple who wanted to adopt her, Madison would just refuse. She was Chloe's mother and needed to do what was best for her baby.

Madison looked at her own mother. She had been supportive of Madison from the first she'd heard of the pregnancy. Madison knew how lucky she had been. Her father was still trying to adjust to the situation and was embarrassed by the whole thing, but he had stood by her too. He hadn't visited her in the hospital, but Madison knew he was busy on the farm. Her brother, Jason, had hugged her and told her it would be all right when he gave her and her mother a ride to the hospital. He had come by once to see the baby, but she knew he was busy with the haying for their family and their neighbors, Frank and Nina.

CHAPTER 6

Mark spent a lot of time working while Abby was gone. He missed her but knew she needed to see her parents. She had only seen them once since Samantha and Amy's funeral, and she was close to her parents.

He also knew there was something bothering Abby. She hadn't told him outright, but they'd been married for enough years that he knew when she was trying to work something out in her mind. She would do that first, usually, and then she would talk to him. He didn't think it was about having a baby. They'd given up trying, and she'd been resigned to the fact that it just wasn't going to happen for them. They had both wanted children. He took a deep breath and let it out. He had even hoped for twins. Since Abby and Samantha were twins, he thought there might be a chance. After several years and no pregnancy, they'd both given up.

While Abby concentrated on her patients, Mark concentrated on moving up in his firm's technology department. He loved coding, so it was no hardship. He thought Abby loved her job at the hospital, but maybe she was looking for something different. It was so hard to let her visit her parents knowing she was struggling with something but not knowing what it was.

He got himself a cup of black coffee and went back to his computer. The project they'd been working on for months was winding down, and he'd be happy to move on to something different. The late hours would end for a while until the next project.

He was looking forward to going to Chokecherry Valley for a few days. He got along well with his in-laws, and he missed Abby. He missed the way they used to talk about everything. He hadn't realized they were growing apart until this trip. It was time for them to start talking again. About everything.

Whatever Abby was dealing with, they would deal with it together. He made a pact with himself to be more aware of their relationship in the future. Starting now.

CHAPTER 7

When Abby and her mother returned to the farm, they pulled into the driveway as Jason was leaving. As their vehicles met side by side, Abby and Jason stopped and each rolled down their windows.

"Hi, Jason," Abby said. "It's good to see you again."

Jason smiled. "I'm sorry to say that I was too young to remember you, but it's good to meet you. Abby? Right?"

"That's right. We'll be running into each other again here at the farm. I'll even help with chores if you need something done."

"That's good to know." He looked across to the passenger seat. "Hi, Nina."

"Hi, Jason. Thanks for coming over and helping. Do you want something to eat before you leave? Or I can wrap something up for you to take?"

"That's okay. I saw some banana bread on the counter and helped myself to that and some milk. I better get home because I'm sure Mom has something cooked."

"Sure. How are Madison and the baby? Has she named her yet?"

Jason's smile widened. "They're fine. The baby's name is Chloe. She's a cute thing. I didn't realize I'd get such a kick out of having a little niece. I've only seen her a little bit because I'm always out in the field, though. They should both be home from the hospital this afternoon. I have too much to do to spend much time with her, though Madison could use the support right now while she decides what to do."

"Well, don't worry about us. If you need to take time off to help her, just let us know," Abby said. "I can do some fieldwork, though you might have to give me a quick refresher before you leave me alone."

Jason grinned. "I'm sure you'd do a fine job and remember how to hay. You just go in a circle or oblong. I didn't realize Frank had you in the field when you were growing up."

"Oh, well we were. My sister and I." She was surprised that she didn't feel more grief at the mention of her sister. She was just remembering the good times they had out in the field. "Sometimes we took turns working in the field. Of course, sometimes we also complained about it." She laughed. "We were normal kids."

"Very normal," Nina said. "You go along Jason. Say hi to your family for us, and we'll come see Chloe and Madison when they get out of the hospital."

"Thanks. I know Madison is afraid of what everyone thinks of her, so that would be kind of you."

"Of course, we'll stand by her," Nina said.

They said their goodbyes, and Jason took off for his second job at home.

As Abby parked the car in front of the farmhouse, she said, "What's going on with Madison that's she's concerned?"

"She's only seventeen." Nina got out of the car, and so did Abby.

Abby was beginning to understand the reason why Jason was so concerned about his sister. "She's still in high school and not married?"

"Right."

"Is she keeping the baby?" Abby asked. The thought crossed her mind that here was a baby who might need a home, but she and Mark had not talked about adopting. Would he be interested? She felt further away from Mark than ever before. They really needed to communicate with each other.

"I don't know. This is the first time Jason has said anything, and I haven't talked to her parents about the subject. They've brought it up, but I didn't push the issue. I've asked them how she's doing when I'm visiting, but it's been just a brief update whenever I said anything. I don't think the boyfriend is in the picture any longer, but I don't know if Madison will keep the baby or put it up for adoption."

"That would be a hard decision for anyone."

They had been walking as they talked and arrived in the kitchen, where Nina started getting lunch ready.

"What can I do to help you with lunch?" Abby asked.

"We're having meatloaf sandwiches, and I have to take one out to your father if he doesn't come in soon." She looked at her smart watch. "He told me this morning that if he wasn't here by one, to bring it out to him."

"I'll go if he isn't back. It's the field Jason started, isn't it?"

"Yes, out east of the house."

"It will give me a chance to get out and see the countryside. I might even take a half-hour drive around, and then I can come back, and we go driving to see the places you think might work for the Meyer family."

"And we can talk about what's bothering you," her mother said as she sliced the meatloaf and stuck it between two slices of bread.

"That too."

They had their own lunch, and Abby's father didn't come home, so she left to drive out to the field. She enjoyed looking out into the vastness of the prairie. There were few trees, and she could see fields for miles around. A few houses dotted the landscape, but otherwise it was fields, roads, and grass. She loved it.

She had missed the quiet when she moved to Houston, but she'd also loved the bustle of a big city. The closest she could come to a nursing job in North Dakota near Chokecherry Valley was in Bismarck. There were two big hospitals there, and she intended to check out the job vacancies there while she was staying at her parents' house. Nurses were in high demand, so she wasn't concerned about openings. She was just curious, and she hadn't talked to Mark yet, she reminded herself.

Her dad was approaching the end of the field where she parked. She got out of the vehicle with his food and went to greet him while watching the mower leave a freshly-cut row of hay behind it. He stopped about fifty feet from her and walked over.

"I was just starting to get hungry."

She handed him the sandwich wrapped in plastic and a thermos of lemonade. "Here I am. We went to Mom's Community Helpers meeting and then had our own lunch."

"So, I'm last." He grinned at her and then took a big bite of his sandwich.

"You wouldn't want us to starve, would you?" she teased him.

He swallowed and took a drink from the thermos. "Of course not. Then I'd have to get my own food."

"Do you want to sit while you're eating?"

"No. I'm fine. I'll be sitting on the mower for a while once I get back on it. I think we're going to have to do something about the seat. I don't remember it being so uncomfortable before."

Abby started to open her mouth, but her dad beat her to it.

"And you can keep quiet about my age, Missy." He grinned again.

"Wouldn't think of saying anything about that, Dad." She smiled back at him.

"So, what did Melissa assign you two to do this morning at the meeting?"

"We're supposed to find a place for the Meyer family to stay until they can either rebuild or find somewhere else to live permanently."

"That's going to be tough around here."

"That's what Mom said. We're going to get Christina to help us."

"She knows the most about the other communities around here, so that's a good choice." Her dad finished his lunch in silence, while Abby looked around at the countryside, feeling a sense of rightness and peace.

Her dad crumpled up the wrapping from the sandwich and handed it to her. "I'll let you throw this away. I'll keep the thermos. Tell your mom the lemonade is really good."

"I will."

He lifted his cap and set it back on his head. "I'll see you this evening. I'm probably going to finish this field, so it might be later."

"That's fine. If you want me to help with the haying, let me know. I'll see you later."

CHAPTER 8

When she got back to the farmhouse, her mom was ready to look at houses for the Meyers. She had called Christina and agreed to pick her up at 3:00 p.m. Until then, they had a few hours to look at three houses her mom thought might be possibilities.

"Brooke is going to come with us when we pick up Christina," her mom said as Abby drove the pickup out of the driveway. "I hope that's okay with you."

"Sure," Abby agreed. "I love children." She hesitated before she added, "I miss Amy. She had such a sweet disposition. I always envied Samantha for having her and not taking care of her better."

Her mother looked out the window on the passenger side, so Abby couldn't see her face. "I miss her too. I always loved buying her purple clothes, because her face would light up with joy." Her voice wobbled.

Abby reached over and squeezed her mother's hand. "You were a wonderful grandmother to her. Maybe you'll be getting some more grandchildren if Paul and Hannah get married."

"I'd love that," said Nina.

Abby looked over at her mom. "I'd like another niece or nephew too. We'll see."

She broke the silence after a moment. "Which direction first?"

Her mom wiped a tear from her eye and said, "Let's go east. There's an old farmhouse out that way that might work. The only problem is that no one's lived in it for a year or so. If it's habitable, we're going to have to get a few cats to take care of the rodents and do some other upkeep. I haven't been out that way for about six months. The owners live in Bismarck and come out occasionally to check it out, but we'll see what it looks like."

"What if we can't get inside?"

"I called one of the owners while you were taking your dad his lunch, and he told me a little secret to get into the house when it's locked." She smiled. "He was a little bit wild in his younger days. But now, from what I can tell, he's settled down with a wife and two kids and a steady job."

"That's good. I'm glad we can get into the house."

When they drove up the driveway, Abby was a little concerned about what they would find inside of the house. The outside of the medium-sized A-frame had peeling paint, the grass was overgrown, and the sidewalk had chipped cement.

"Well," her mother said. "We'll just have to see the inside before deciding."

Nina carefully walked along the cement steps and reached for the front doorknob. It turned but didn't open. She walked to the side of the house and found a little gnome stuck into the dirt. She pulled and tugged it out of the dirt. She turned it upside down, and there was a piece of duct tape covering a hollowed-out hole. She pulled at the edge of the tape, and a key dropped out of the hole. She left the gnome where she'd found it.

When they stepped into the house, Abby put her hand over her nose. "Well, you were right about the rodents."

She looked around at the bare living room. The carpet was stained with droppings and footprints from someone walking through the house in the winter or perhaps other wet weather. She looked up at the ceiling to see that it looked intact and okay to live with after a fresh coat of paint. The walls could use some paint too, but otherwise looked okay. There was no warping of the drywall that she could see.

They moved into the kitchen, and it looked similarly intact. It was dated, but not in bad shape with a little sprucing up. "This doesn't look too bad down here."

Her mother nodded. "No, so far, so good. Let's check out the bathroom and then the bedrooms upstairs."

The rest of the house was livable, but there were only two bedrooms and the only bathroom was downstairs. The upstairs just had the bedrooms. They inspected the ceiling, and there didn't appear to be any leaks that they could see.

They relocked the front door and replaced the key.

"This one would work if we can't find anything bigger. They could split the kids' bedroom into two rooms. It's pretty big. The house is about five miles from Chokecherry Valley, and the plows come out this way in the winter. I'm guessing the busing for school would be okay."

"Sounds like it would be okay, but we've just started looking." Abby pulled out of the driveway, and they went to look at the other two properties they knew about. Just from glancing at the outside, they knew that neither one would work. One was just too small, and the other one had a hole in the roof they could see from the road.

Her mother looked at her smart watch. "We have just enough time to pick up Christina and Brooke."

Abby remembered the way to their place, even though it had been years since she'd been there. "Why is Brooke staying with Christina? Is there something wrong with Kym that Brooke isn't with her?"

"When Kym got her divorce, she and her ex-husband basically dumped Brooke. It's sad. Christina is looking at adopting Brooke, so Kym can't come back later and take her away. Christina thinks Brooke has had enough trauma in her young life."

"That's sad about Kym, but it's a good thing Christina loves Brooke so much she'd adopt her."

"She feels she might be too old, but she said she loves Brooke and will do anything she can for her."

"That's great." Abby was thinking about Brooke and about Jason's niece, Chloe. Two little girls who needed a permanent home. Her throat closed with longing. Why couldn't she and Mark have a little girl of their own? Why was it so hard? She didn't know why God had made it impossible for her to get pregnant. At first, she and Mark hadn't been concerned, but as time went on and nothing happened, they both got tested. There seemed to be no reason for the lack of pregnancy. They just didn't have any children. She shut off the thoughts as she pulled into Christina's driveway.

Brooke and Christina were sitting on the front step with Brooke's car seat beside them. The white house behind them had dark green shutters. The place looked like someone had recently painted the exterior. It was a beautiful summer day, with the birds singing and the sun shining.

Christina stood up as Brooke came running over to Abby. "We're going to ride with you."

Abby smiled down at her. "That's terrific. We'll be going for a long drive. Are you ready?"

"Grandma said I could bring my book and my tablet to play with in the pickup. Is that okay?" Brooke asked anxiously.

"That's perfect. It will give you something to do when we're busy talking."

"I need my car seat. I'm too little to sit in a pickup without it."

"Your grandma is bringing it over. You get to sit in the back seat."

"Will you sit with me?"

"Sure. My mom can drive, and your grandma can sit in front, and they can talk while we talk."

"I don't talk much," Brooke said.

Abby was charmed by the little girl. She was a mixture of shyness, sweetness, and seriousness. "You just look at your book and tablet, and if you talk, I'll talk. Otherwise, I'll just listen to your grandma and my mom."

Brooke smiled back at her. "Okay."

They settled in the back seat, with Brooke in her car seat, and Abby beside her. Christina and Nina took their places in the front seat.

Christina started directing Nina to the first house to look at. The afternoon was warm but not overly hot, as long as they didn't sit in the car without the air-conditioning. Abby felt herself relax and started enjoying the day. Since it was the end of June, there were plenty of wildflowers to see among the grasses lining the road. She saw some sunflowers, wild prairie roses, and even a few bluebells.

Abby had become so used to Houston and people everywhere, that this quiet was a welcome change. Her thoughts about moving out of Houston returned. It wasn't that she wanted to move back to Chokecherry Valley where she grew up, but she did want to live in a smaller city than Houston. She thought about finding a nursing job in Bismarck. Her brother-in-law Paul worked at one of the hospitals, and he seemed to like it.

She thought about Paul and what her mom and dad had told her about his living with them for a few months. It sounded like he'd had a bad time after his wife and daughter's deaths. Even though she was mad at Paul for the lifestyle he and Sam had lived, she felt sorry for him. She missed her twin, and she could only imagine what Paul was going through with both his wife and daughter gone at the same time. Abby knew she'd have to get over her anger at Paul. Her mom had already invited him and his girlfriend, Hannah, over for supper tomorrow night. She was not looking forward to it.

She wondered what Hannah was like. Her own sister had been outgoing and always wanted to wear the latest styles and had her hair perfect. Except when she was drunk. Abby winced.

"Are you okay?" Brooke asked. "You made a funny noise."

Abby looked over and saw Brooke watching her with serious eyes and puckered lips. Abby smiled at her. "I'm fine. Just clearing my throat."

"Oh. I do that when I have a cold." The little girl watched her solemnly. "Do you have a cold?"

"No, I don't. Just a tickle in my throat."

Brooke put her hand to her throat and moved her fingers along her neck. "I can't tickle my throat."

Abby laughed, and it felt good. "You can't tickle your own throat. It just happens."

"Oh."

"We're here," Christina announced from the front seat.

Abby unbuckled Brooke from her car seat, and then opened her own door to get out of the vehicle.

Brooke climbed over the car seat and out the same door as Abby. They stood there looking around.

Abby thought the house seemed in better shape than the ones she had looked at with her mother earlier.

"Well," Christina said. "A little work on the outside might be necessary. It doesn't look too bad. Now for the inside."

The owners of the big, rambling ranch house had left the front door unlocked. It looked like certain parts of the house had been added at different times, but the L-shaped house appeared to be in pretty good shape except for the need for a coat or two of paint. The roof looked fairly new, and the front door looked like it had been replaced recently.

They went inside, with Christina holding Brooke back while Nina and Abby took the lead. The entryway was a mudroom with a sink and a place to hang coats and put boots or shoes.

"Nina, why don't you and Abby go see if we have any visitors here before I bring Brooke in any further?" Christina said.

Abby led her mother out of the mudroom into the kitchen. There didn't seem to be any animals or rodents that Abby could detect. She didn't smell any disuse either. She wondered how long the house had been uninhabited. She and her mother made a quick tour through the house and determined it was okay for Brooke. They rejoined Christina, and Nina nodded. "No problems."

Christina took Brooke by the shoulders and squatted down. "Don't touch anything, honey. We're just looking, okay?"

"Okay." Brooke had her serious face on again, and Abby felt her heart tug. The little girl needed a lot more fun in her life. Did she have any kids her own age to play with during the day?

They began to view the house and walked through the living room, downstairs bathroom, and kitchen. It all looked outdated but was in good shape otherwise. The upstairs was the same. There were three bedrooms and a bathroom. It actually seemed like the place would work for the family to move into until they had their bearings and decided if they wanted to stay in Chokecherry Valley or move elsewhere.

Nina was smiling at Christina when they met up in the kitchen again a short time later. "This certainly looks like it should work for them. What do you think?"

"I agree. We can get some volunteers to paint the outside of the house. The inside will need a thorough cleaning, but it's livable otherwise. I'll call the owners and see what kind of a deal I can make for the Meyer family to rent for six months. That's the time frame they gave me when I suggested we help them find a place."

"We need to check out the electrical and plumbing before we move any further. Let's have Frank figure out that part and who to call if he can't do it himself."

"I'll give you the owners' information when we get back to the pickup, and he can talk to them. If it's all okay, I'll bring the Meyer family out here to take a look and see what they think," Christina said.

"Sounds good to me."

Abby looked down at Brooke. "Let's get you back into your car seat and back home. You look like you could use a snack."

"I'm hungry," Brooke agreed.

"I have some juice and crackers in my bag in the pickup. You can look in there for them, Abby. I don't have any secrets in that bag." Christina smiled, and her face relaxed for the first time that day.

Abby realized how Christina was just as solemn as Brooke, and she wondered if caring for Brooke was taking a toll on Christina.

When Brooke was settled with her juice box and crackers, Abby joined her mom and Christina outside the house where they were studying the front steps.

"Just doing one last look before we head home," her mom said.

"Would you like me to watch Brooke for you tomorrow when you bring the Meyer family out here? I could take her over and meet Jason's new niece. I'd like to see the baby too," Abby told them.

"That's a good idea," Nina said. "I know that Madison is worried about what everyone thinks, and she could use some younger company. I'll call her mom and see if Madison is up for company. I know she was just getting out of the hospital today."

"We won't stay long," Abby said. "I just thought Brooke might like to see a little baby. Most kids like to see someone smaller than them."

Christina patted Abby's arm. "Thank you. That's a good idea. Since Brooke and I have been together this last year, she hasn't seen many kids. I intend to do something about that, but I seem to keep getting pulled into these projects, and my health isn't what it used to be."

"I'll be happy to watch Brooke anytime you want help while I'm here for the next few weeks. My husband, Mark, will be coming to stay part of next week, but he won't mind. He loves children too."

The drive back to Christina's house passed quickly. Brooke fell asleep in her car seat, and Nina and Christina talked quietly in the front seat. Abby wondered about Madison's baby. What had Jason meant by not getting to see his niece for very long. Was Madison giving her baby up for adoption? Abby really needed to talk to Mark when she got back to her parents' farmhouse.

"That was a productive day," Nina said when they were on their own again driving back to the farm. "Two options for the Meyer family, though I think they'll choose that second house. The first was just too small, unless they have no other option."

"I agree. It's nice of you to help out with this, Mom. You and Dad always help others. It's a good lesson you taught us growing up. I don't feel like I help people much anymore, though."

"Of course you do. There's your work at the hospital. I'm sure you've helped hundreds of people."

"It seems so impersonal."

"I'm sure they feel like you care when you're treating them."

"I try to make them feel better, but then they leave. It's in and out. I want someone to take care of all the time."

Nina laughed. "Maybe. But once you're taking care of someone all the time, you might get tired of it."

Abby laughed too. "You're right. But I still want it. Mark and I have been trying to have a baby for years, and it just hasn't happened. I had finally given up on the idea."

"Is that why you came to stay at Chokecherry for two weeks?"

"Partly. Of course, I wanted to spend more time with you and Dad, but lately, I just needed to get away from Houston. Let's say I'm doing both at the same time. It is so peaceful out on the farm with you and Dad, though. I'm glad I came here instead of going to some hotel or bed-and-breakfast to think."

"I'm glad you came, too."

Nina was pulling into the driveway when Abby asked the question her mind had been trying to brush aside all day. She felt like a bad person for obsessing about Madison and her baby. "Do you think Madison is going to give her baby up for adoption? You know her parents, Gary and Patricia. Have they said anything?"

Nina put the pickup gear shift into park and shut off the engine. She looked at Abby. "Patricia mentioned adoption, but I have no idea what Madison thinks of the idea since she had the baby. I don't know if Patricia has talked to her about it. Sometimes when someone has a child though, and they hold that baby in their arms, they don't want to give it up. I don't want to discourage you, but you might want to take this slow. I don't want you to be hurt if you set your heart on adopting and Madison isn't interested."

Abby looked down at her hands where she was twisting them in her lap. "I've wanted a baby for so long. I feel bad thinking about Madison's baby when she must be going through a very bad time trying to decide what to do."

She looked back up at her mother. "But if this is God giving me a baby, I don't want to miss the opportunity. Mark and I haven't even discussed adoption. I know we should have, but it's only recently we've come to the realization that we're not going to have our own child. We just haven't had the adoption discussion. And when I came to Chokecherry Valley, I wasn't even really thinking about adopting. I had just left my job in Houston. Something I haven't told Mark about either. There are just so many thoughts in my mind, decisions I need to make. A baby wasn't among those decisions."

Abby grimaced. "I guess a baby is now at the top of my discussion list with Mark. I need to call him tonight and talk to him."

"It sounds like the two of you have a lot to discuss."

Abby groaned. "I really wanted to talk to him in person, but if Madison is seriously considering giving up the baby, I need to talk to Mark now and not wait. I guess a phone conversation is going to have to do for now."

"Let's eat supper, and then you can talk to him. I'll take care of Dad's meal whenever he gets in from the field. It'll be okay."

"Thanks, Mom."

CHAPTER 9

Abby wasn't looking forward to the conversation with Mark. She had really wanted to get her thoughts in order, and then talk to him in person, but that didn't seem to be the way this was going to happen. She would just have to go with the flow and take things with Mark one thing at a time. Was this God's timing? It was certainly different than hers would have been. She smiled wryly. Things happened when they happened. She should know that by now.

She dialed the number and listened to it ring. After two rings, Mark picked up.

"Hi, Honey," Mark said. "I miss you."

"I miss you too." Abby suddenly felt tears coming and sniffed.

Mark must have noticed, because he said, "Are you okay?"

She sniffed again. "Sorry. I'm just so happy to hear your voice, and I wish you were here. So much has happened that I don't even know where to start."

"What? You've only been there a day and a half. What on earth could have happened in such a short amount of time? Are your parents okay?"

"Yes, they are doing well. Dad's out in the field right now, and Mom's downstairs reading a book. She's finally relaxing a little while she waits for Dad to come back."

"That's good. I'm nearly done with that project. We're finishing earlier than planned. I'm mostly working from home the next few days, and I'll actually have the weekend off. I think I'll go golfing. What's going on there that's keeping you so busy?"

Abby wished she could see Mark's face. His brown eyes would be so full of love and understanding, and that's what she needed right now. She didn't want him so far away. "Mom and Dad have a hired hand. He comes early in the morning and is gone by noon. His name is Jason, and his family lives next door."

"You mean the next farm over?" Mark asked. He came from country roots also and knew next door didn't mean the same thing as it did in the city.

"That's right. He's a few years younger than me, so I never really knew him growing up. He has a sister Madison who is seventeen. She just had a baby." Abby stopped there with the story. She wasn't sure how to broach a possible adoption with Mark.

"Is she going to keep the baby?" He asked immediately with no hesitation. Almost as if he knew that's what she wanted to know.

"I don't know. Mom says adoption has been mentioned. What do you think about us adopting a baby, Mark? I know we never talked about it, and we should have at least brought it up. I don't know how you feel about it, and I should know. We've been trying for years to have a baby, and it's just not happening. I wasn't thinking about adoption when I came here. I had other things on my mind, but now I can't stop thinking about that little girl and what might become of her. I want to adopt. If not her, then another baby. What do you think about all this?"

There was a long pause, and Abby gave him time. It was a lot to take in.

"First," Mark said, "I think we should have done a face-to-face chat on our phones for this conversation, since we couldn't have it in person."

"I never thought of that, but you're right." Abby frowned. Of course Mark would think of the technological solution. It would have been better than just a phone conversation.

"Second, I'm coming to Chokecherry Valley as soon as I can get my ticket changed. I think we need to be together for this discussion."

"Oh, Mark." She started crying.

"It's okay, honey. It's going to be fine. We'll work this out."

The tears slowed, and she got up from the bed where she'd been sitting to get a tissue. "Just a second. I need to wipe my eyes." She set down the phone, wiped her eyes and nose, and went back to the phone. "I'm back."

"Are you okay?"

"I'm so happy you're coming here, but don't you have to go into the office?"

"Like I said. Things are winding down. I can do everything from home, so I can do it from the farm."

"That's great. I can't wait to see you. Text me when you have the new flight, and I'll come pick you up."

"That won't be necessary. I think we're going to need our own vehicles to get around. I'll rent something when I get to Bismarck."

That sounded promising. Maybe he wanted to go see the baby and was seriously thinking about adoption. "Do you need time to think about adoption, Mark? Am I being too pushy?"

She heard Mark sigh.

"I've thought about it for a while, but you didn't seem to be planning any further than having our own baby, so I was waiting for you to be ready. It seems like you're ready now."

"I am. I don't know what will happen with Madison's baby, but I am willing to adopt."

"Then I think we should both do some more thinking on the subject, and I'll be there in the next day or two so we can talk together. Do you think you can keep busy during that time?"

"Definitely. There's a family who lost their house and belongings in a fire. We're getting a house ready for them to move into, and Mom's friend Christina is taking care of her four-year-old granddaughter, Brooke. She's so cute. I'm going to be watching her some of the time when she can't be with Christina and Mom, because of the work they're doing."

Mark laughed. "Sounds like you have plenty to keep you occupied."

"I might even take Brooke over to see Madison's baby. Are you okay with that?"

"That's fine, Abby. Do what makes you happy. We'll work it all out when I get there."

When they hung up a few minutes later, Abby was happier and more settled. Mark seemed okay with adopting a baby. If not Madison's, at least he would consider another baby.

She wondered how long Mark had been thinking about adoption, waiting for her to be ready. He was definitely a keeper in the husband department. She smiled, but it didn't last long. She still hadn't told Mark she had quit her job at the Houston hospital and wanted to find something different. A lot would depend on how things went with Madison and her baby. That could change their whole life plan. Maybe if they didn't live in Houston, she could stay home with the baby for a while before going back to work.

She was happy he was coming to Chokecherry sooner than planned. They'd have more time together to talk about a lot of things they probably should have discussed already. It didn't do any good to push hard topics aside. They were always still there waiting to be dealt with sooner or later.

She went downstairs to tell her mom that Mark was going to be visiting sooner than planned. She knew her mom would be happy for her.

CHAPTER 10

The next morning Abby got up early to help her mom in the garden. The June day promised to be hot, and they wanted to get out and weed as early as possible. The summer breeze brought the scent of lilacs. There were some late-blooming purple lilacs on the bushes near the garden. Her mother had also planted some marigolds, petunias, and pansies that she got at the grocery store. She said that she couldn't wait for the flowers to grow and bloom. She wanted the plants already started, so they would bloom earlier in the season.

They worked on the carrot and radish patch and planned to get the onions and beans done before they went to visit Madison and her baby, Chloe. Nina had called Patricia the evening before and asked if they were up for company. Patricia said it would be a good idea, since Madison seemed to be sinking into some kind of depression and needed something to focus on besides deciding what to do about the baby. Christina had agreed to visit and bring Brooke with her. She thought the four-year-old would help lighten the atmosphere.

Abby changed into shorts and a white T-shirt to visit Madison and Patricia. She slipped on sneakers and was ready to go. She was trying to decide whether or not to mention to Madison and Patricia that she and Mark wanted to adopt a baby. She just couldn't decide what to say and chose to wait and see if there was a good opportunity. Mark would be angry at her if she said anything without him present, but she didn't really want to wait. She felt an urgent need to speak up and tell Madison she was interested in adopting Chloe.

Abby was driving, and she glanced at her mom before looking back out at the road. She had told her mom about part of the conversation she'd had with Mark. "Did you mention to Patricia that Mark and I might be interested in adopting a baby?"

"No. I really think it's best for you and Mark to bring it up with Madison. Patricia did say that Madison was considering adoption but also said that since the baby was born, it's hard to talk to Madison. She's depressed and tired. I'm sure her hormones are fluctuating. It's hard being a new mother. Plus, she's young and trying to make a hard decision."

"I agree. It must be difficult." Abby wondered what it would be like to have her own child. It looked as if that wasn't God's plan for her, so she'd never know about fluctuating hormones. If she got to adopt, maybe she'd at least know what it was like to be a mother. She had hope for the first time in a long time.

It was around 10:00 a.m. when they drove into the Allmen's yard. Christina was just pulling into the driveway too. Brooke was waving eagerly at Abby, and she waved back.

"Brooke is really taken with you," Nina said.

Abby smiled at her mom. "I love that little girl. She is so sweet. I bet she'll make Madison feel better."

They all went up to the doorway together, where Patricia stood to greet them. Somewhere in the bustle of entering the house, Abby found that Brooke had slipped her hand into Abby's hand. It was a good thing that Nina was the one carrying the quilt she'd made for the baby, and she also carried the two jars of chokecherry jelly that she'd brought over for Patricia.

"Are you excited to see the little baby?" Abby asked Brooke.

"Yes. Grandma said her name is Chloe, and I might get to hold her if Madison lets me," Brooke said proudly.

"That would be nice."

"There she is," Brooke said.

Madison was sitting on the couch with Chloe in her lap. There was a blanket, pacifier, and some baby toys scattered on the sofa on either side of her. She smiled at them all, but Abby noticed the tired droop to her eyelids. They would have to keep this visit short. She felt a twinge of disappointment that she wouldn't get to speak with Madison alone and see if she was still considering giving the baby up for adoption. She chastised herself for thinking more about her own wants than Madison's needs. But Chloe was so cute. Abby couldn't believe the possibility that this baby might be her own daughter if Madison would give her up for adoption.

Chloe had her eyes at half-mast and seemed content.

Brooke tugged on Abby's hand. "Can I hold her now?"

Abby looked at Madison. "Hi. I'm Abby. I saw your brother the other day when he came over to help my dad, Frank, with the haying."

Madison smiled shyly. "Hi. Jason mentioned seeing you. I remember you from when you lived at your parents' house."

"Brooke would like to hold the baby. Are you okay with that?" Behind her, she was aware that Patricia was talking quietly with Christina and her mom.

"Sure." Madison struggled to sit on the edge of the couch. She pushed the baby toys and other things off to the side and gestured to Brooke. "Why don't you come sit here on the couch, so you can hold the baby." She smiled as Brooke got up onto the couch and held out her arms.

"Why don't we just set Chloe in your lap?" Abby sat on the couch, with Brooke between her and Madison.

Madison set the baby in Brooke's lap and held Chloe's head, while Brooke rested one hand on Chloe's tummy.

"Look, Grandma," Brooke said to Christina. "I'm holding Chloe."

The baby's eyes seemed to open wider as she stared at Brooke.

"See. She's looking at me."

Everyone in the room laughed to see the two together.

"I need to get a picture of this," Christina said, pulling her phone out of her jean's pocket. She snapped a few pictures, and then said to Brooke. "I think it might be someone else's turn to hold Chloe."

Brooke frowned, but then smiled when Abby said, "How about me? You can stay here next to me while I hold her."

Madison withdrew her arm from under Chloe's head when she was assured that Abby had a good grip on the baby. She flexed her arm. "She is heavier than she looks."

Abby stared down at Chloe. She was such a cute little thing in her pink onesie and with her serene expression. Chloe closed her eyes and sighed.

"She does that all the time," Madison said. "The first time she sighed, I was worried. She kept doing it, and then I got used to it."

"She's very cute. You're doing a wonderful job," Abby told her.

"Thank you."

Abby thought she detected a note of tears in Madison's words, but other than biting her lip, Madison didn't say anything else.

The other women had been watching and then gone back to talking about the Community Helpers project for the Meyer family.

"They decided to take that house we looked at yesterday," Christina said. "Melissa is getting volunteers to paint and clean."

"Frank had the volunteer electricians and plumbers out there yesterday, and everything looked fine to them," Nina said.

"Well, that's one thing off our to-do list, but there is a lot more to getting them set up," Christina agreed.

"Did the flyers get put up for donations? I can help with that. Madison and I could drive

around and put some of them up," Patricia
volunteered.

"I'd like to do that," Madison said. "I need
to get out of the house for a bit. Besides the
hospital, I haven't been anywhere for a while."

"Do you want to take Chloe with us?"
Patricia asked.

Madison shrugged. "Sure. Why not?"

"Okay. That sounds like fun," Patricia said.
"I'll call Melissa and see what's going on with that,
and she'll let us know what to do."

Abby looked at the other women. "Who's
next?" she asked, even though she wanted to keep
holding Chloe. She could hold her all day.

Christina took the baby from Abbey, and
Brooke followed her grandmother around the living
room as Christina cooed and swayed with the baby
as she paced the living room.

"Do you want to go outside, Madison?"
Abby asked. "It's a really beautiful day."

Madison got up. "I'd love to. Mom said the
yard looks summery today with the birds singing on
the lawn by the bird feeder. I haven't had the energy
since I got home from the hospital, but it would be
great to get outside for a bit."

"Well, I think you have plenty of babysitters
right now," Abby said as they went out the front
door together and left the other women with Chloe.

Madison blinked as she stepped outside.
"It's bright. Yeah. I don't like to leave Chloe with
my mom too much. She's done so much already."

Abby heard the tears in the teen's voice
again. Her mom was right. Lots of hormones and
emotions going on with Madison. "Let's sit on

those chairs." Abby pointed to two chairs that were close enough to the bird feeders for them to watch if they remained still so they wouldn't scare the birds.

They sat down, and Madison sighed. "I wish…"

Abby waited, but she didn't continue. "I'm only going to be here for two weeks, and then I'll be gone. If you want to talk about something I can keep it to myself. I won't tell my mom, so you don't need to worry that it'll get back to your mom."

"I just feel like such a burden to my mom. She's helping me take care of Chloe, and she doesn't complain, but it just makes me feel guilty that I'm adding more work for her." Madison took a deep breath and let it out.

"Your mom seems to be doing fine," Abby said. "She loves you and only wants to help you."

Madison started crying, and Abby got up and placed a hand around Madison's shoulders. "It's okay. I heard you might give Chloe up for adoption."

Madison only cried harder.

Abby just patted her on the shoulder as Madison pulled some tissues out of her pocket. The fact that she was prepared with tissues gave Abby a clue as to how often the tears came. Maybe if she came straight to the point about adoption, it would help Madison talk about the situation. "What's bothering you about adoption?"

"I want to keep Chloe," she blurted out. "I just don't want to burden Mom if I keep Chloe, and I know it will be a lot of extra work for her, and I don't know how it would work. I don't want to give her up. She's mine." The tears continued, and Abby just let her cry. Eventually, the tears stopped, and Madison just sat there breathing heavily.

Abby moved away. "I'm going to let you sit here for a few minutes while I go keep the others in the house for a little bit. How about I come back in ten minutes and see how you are?"

"Thank you," Madison looked up at her. "I don't want them to know."

"Okay. I won't tell anyone, but I would suggest that you let your mom know. I think she'll be on your side. She loves Chloe too. She would probably be happy to help you raise her."

Madison shrugged and looked down. "I don't know," she whispered.

Abby patted her on the shoulder and went back into the house, her own heart hurting for herself and for Madison. It looked like Chloe was not going to be the baby for her and Mark. She really thought that Chloe should be staying with Madison, which was a good thing for both of them.

CHAPTER 11

When Abby and her mom arrived back at the farm after their visit with Madison and Patricia, there was an SUV parked in the driveway. "Do you know who is here?"

Her mom shook her head. "The vehicle doesn't look familiar."

Abby noticed a rental sticker. "It's Mark. He's here already. Why didn't he text me that he'd be here so soon?"

"Have you looked at your phone lately?"

Abby pulled her phone out of the holder in the front of the pickup. "I guess I left it here in the pickup when we went into Patricia's house."

She looked at the incoming texts and saw she'd missed a few from Mark. He must have texted earlier that morning when she was sleeping, and then again when he arrived in Bismarck. She didn't know how she missed the early morning text. She couldn't remember if she'd even looked at her phone that morning. She thought it was a habit to at least glance at it, but she couldn't remember.

Mark came out of the house to meet them.

"Hi, Nina," he said to her mom.

"Hi, Mark." She gave him a hug and then said, "I'm going into the house. You two can talk."

"Thank you." He watched until the door closed behind her, and then he turned to Abby. "Hi, Honey."

She hugged him, and he hugged her back. "It's so good to see you. I didn't expect you so soon, and I must have forgotten to look at my phone this morning."

He continued to hold her. "Could that be because you were going to see that little baby?"

She looked up at him from the shelter of his arms and saw he was smiling. She did get wrapped up in things and forget. She nodded. "I think so. I really wanted her to be the one. When you said you were ready to adopt, it just seemed like it was meant to be."

She stepped out of his embrace and took his hand. "I'm happy you came early. I'm kind of bummed right now."

"What's going on?"

She led him over to the front steps. "Let's sit down, and I'll fill you in."

They sat down on the top step, and he took her hand in his. "What's up?"

"Mom and I just came back from visiting Madison and her baby, Chloe. Madison's mom, Patricia, was there. So were Christina and her four-year-old granddaughter, Brooke. We spent some time visiting, and then just Madison and I went outside to talk. I meant to bring up that you and I were interested in adopting, but before I could say anything, she burst into tears and told me she wants to keep the baby. Of course, I couldn't say anything at that point, so we talked a little bit, and I told her to tell her mom that she wanted to keep the baby. Madison is afraid it's too much of a burden for her family to help her."

Mark leaned over and kissed her on the top of her head. "I'm sorry. What do you think is going to happen?"

"I think she's going to keep the baby. I think once she tells her mom, Patricia will do what she can to help Madison. I don't think Chloe is the baby for us."

Mark gave her a hug. "We've just started talking about adopting. Maybe it's just too soon. We'll find a little one to add to our family. I know you're disappointed now, but let's not give up hope already."

"You're right. I can get rather impatient."

Mark laughed. "How about very impatient?"

Abby laughed too. "Let's not start an argument right away. You just got here. Let's wait until later."

Mark squeezed her hand and got up, pulling her with him. "Let's go find your mom and get some food. I'm hungry."

"Me too. It's been a long morning."

CHAPTER 12

Abby spent the rest of the day helping her mom in the garden and catching up on household chores. Mark worked remotely on his work project trying to finish it up by the weekend.

The next morning, Friday, Mark continued working, and Abby and her mom went to Chokecherry Valley to St. Anne's Church to see the secretary, Melissa. She had the plans for the Meyer family.

Abby planned to go shopping with Mark in Bismarck after lunch. They were going to buy supplies for the Meyer family, and she needed to know what they should be getting to help out the family. She knew one of the other Community Helpers members had already taken the family shopping, so she wanted to know what the best things to buy would be.

She was looking forward to getting into Bismarck and spending the day with Mark. Between his work and her helping her mother and working on the Community Helpers project, she hadn't seen much of him since he arrived. They planned to eat lunch with her parents and then go to the city for shopping.

She was also happy to be busy with Mark, because she was nervous about seeing Paul and his girlfriend that evening. Her mother had invited them for supper. Abby wasn't sure how she felt about her brother-in-law dating so soon after Sam's death. He deserved to be happy, but she still held a grudge about how much drinking Paul had done with Sam during the early part of their marriage before Paul got clean. She knew intellectually the accident that killed Sam wasn't Paul's fault, but she still had a lot of mixed feelings that she couldn't seem to sort out over the whole ordeal.

She wasn't sure why she was still holding a grudge against him. He had had a problem with drinking, which he had gotten help for. He tried to get Sam to accept help, but she didn't. That was what Abby was having a hard time understanding. Why didn't Sam get help? She had a good husband and a lovely little girl. Why didn't she get help and stop drinking? Abby knew her anger should be directed at Sam and not Paul, and she shouldn't really be angry anyway. It was sad that Sam didn't get help before it was too late, and she'd died in that accident.

Maybe it wasn't the drinking so much as the jealousy Abby was feeling over Sam's blessing at having Amy. She didn't understand why Sam was able to get pregnant, and she wasn't. That's what she was really angry about. She finally admitted it. She was angry and jealous that Sam had had no trouble having Amy, and she threw it all away by her drinking.

Somehow, she was going to have to learn how to live with her feelings. Maybe once she and Mark were able to adopt a child, some of her jealousy would disappear. She didn't want to be angry at Sam. She missed her. She'd missed her for a long time even before she died. That was the other part of the equation. She missed the Sam she'd grown up with before the drinking started. And she blamed Paul for Sam starting to drink, and that wasn't fair to Paul. She'd come back to some circular thinking. It was time to go shopping with Mark.

She went into her bedroom and dressed in jeans and a button-down, short-sleeved shirt. She slipped some comfortable sandals on her feet, as they would be doing a lot of walking for the afternoon while they shopped. She stuffed the list from Melissa into her purse and headed downstairs to see if Mark was ready to leave.

Mark had finished working on his project, and since it was Friday, he said he wouldn't work anymore today or during the weekend unless a problem came up. Since they were shopping, and then having company that evening, he had needed to finish before they left.

When she got to the dining room, where he had set up for the morning, she saw he was on his phone.

"Right," he said into the phone. "Ten-thirty a.m., Monday. Tuesday's the Fourth of July, so we won't be doing anything that day."

He listened for another minute, and then said. "I'm taking off the Fourth and the rest of next week. You can call or text if there's a problem, and I'll work on it. Otherwise, I'm here in North Dakota spending time with my wife's family."

There was another pause. "Okay. Bye." He pressed the end button.

Abby had stood waiting for him to finish. "Was that your boss?"

"Yes. As you heard, there's a meeting Monday morning that I'll attend remotely. Then I'll finish up a few things and take vacation time. That should work out well. I'm done for today and this weekend."

"Good. Then we can leave in about fifteen minutes, if that's okay with you?" she asked.

"That's fine. Let me finish up one quick email, clean off the table, and we'll take off for the city."

"I'm going to tell Mom we're leaving and see if there's anything she needs us to pick up in Bismarck. I forgot to ask her earlier."

Abby found her mom sorting through some papers that were spread across the coffee table by the living room couch. "You look busy."

"Just trying to get a handle on all this paperwork Melissa gave me for the Meyer project. Thank goodness it's just copies, because I'm getting them all mixed up."

"I can help you tomorrow. Right now, Mark's finishing up a few things, and then we're leaving for Bismarck. Did you want me to bring you anything?"

"No, we're fine. Your dad and I did a little shopping the day we picked you up from the airport, so there's nothing more to do. I'm going to bake a pie for this evening and look at these papers. Your dad should be done with the haying in that field by four. I think he'll just stop there for the day."

"That sounds good."

"Your dad is really looking forward to seeing Paul and Hannah again. I know you have some reservations about Paul, but he was really good for Dad when he helped us this spring."

"I know, Mom. I'll be nice. I'm really trying to see his side of things. I just miss Sam and Amy, and I want someone to blame."

Her mother got up and hugged her. "You know in your heart who's to blame. Let's just let forgiveness be our focus, and remember the love and joy we had with Amy and Sam. We can't change anything."

Abby hugged her back. "I'm working on it, Mom. Like I said. I promise to be good this evening. I won't scream and yell at him."

"Good. I know you're going to like Hannah."

Abby thought about that and realized she really did want to like Hannah. None of what had happened involved her.

CHAPTER 13

It felt good to get out of her parents' house for a while. She enjoyed seeing them, but there were a lot of memories of Sam and Amy in all the rooms. She wasn't as fragile as she'd been when she was there for the funeral, but still. It was sometimes difficult when a memory caught her off guard.

She understood her mother's apprehension about Abby and Paul in the same room again. She hadn't seen him since the funeral, when she had screamed at him, Abby claimed that the accident was his fault. Paul hadn't even been in the vehicle when it crashed.

She smiled as Mark drove to Bismarck. It was good to spend some time alone with him. Before she'd come to Chokecherry Valley, he had been wrapped up in his project at work, and then as soon as he got to Chokecherry, they discussed adoption. This felt more relaxed.

"We've got a long list for today. Are you ready?" Abby asked.

"Definitely. It will feel good to be walking around instead of sitting at a desk or table all day long. What do we have to buy?"

"It's just a lot of household things. As much as we can fit into the SUV. I told Melissa we're donating everything we buy today. I hope that's okay with you." She didn't anticipate Mark objecting.

"Hey, that's great." He smiled at her before returning his attention to the road. "I'm glad you thought of it."

"Thanks for being so understanding. About everything."

"You mean the adoption too?"

"Yes. I told Mom we're considering it, and I'm sure she told Dad."

"That's okay. I expected that."

"I don't think Madison's baby is the one for us." Abby sighed. "I know that would have been too easy."

"Don't give up yet. She may change her mind. And we just started the process. It can take a long time."

"I know. I'm just happy we're talking about it. Would you be willing to adopt an older child?" She was thinking that she'd be okay with a young child instead of a baby, but what would Mark think?

"That might be harder to do. They already might have known their mom or dad. I'm not sure about that. I'd have to think about it. I'm not totally opposed to adopting a child, but a lot would depend on the circumstances of the child."

They talked of other things after that and enjoyed their time in Bismarck. They stopped midway through the afternoon and chatted over coffee. Abby felt like she was on a date with her husband. She still hadn't told him about leaving her job in Houston. Maybe on their way back to the farm she would tell him. She didn't want to ruin the rest of her afternoon with him.

In the end, she didn't say anything to Mark about her job. Adoptions could be expensive, and she might need to beg for her nursing job back in Houston until an adoption was finalized. She could manage staying at the job if she knew something good would come of it.

CHAPTER 14

As the time for Paul and Hannah's arrival neared, Abby moved around the kitchen and fidgeted.

Nina finally put a hand on her arm. "Calm down. It's just Paul and Hannah. It will be okay."

"I know," Abby said. "But I have to apologize to Paul for the nasty things I said to him at the funeral. Screaming at him at the graveside. I can't believe I did that." She squeezed her eyes shut and then opened them. "What was I thinking?"

"We all do things we wish we could undo. Paul will understand. Just tell him you're not angry with him anymore, and he'll forgive you. I think you'll find that Samantha's and Amy's deaths have changed him a lot."

"I would expect they would change him. I hope for the better." Abby regretted that last bit but couldn't take it back.

"You've always had a grudge against him since he and Samantha married. Maybe it's time you thought about why that is." Her mother held up her hand before Abby could say anything. "And no, it wasn't his drinking that upset you so much. Just think about it."

"It was his drinking. I think it led to Sam drinking more." She saw her mother was going to say something, and she beat her to it. "But I will consider there is another reason and think about it. Maybe then I can get past it."

"Maybe you can. And if you need help, I'll tell you why you were so mad at him," her mother said irrepressibly.

Abby laughed. "I'll let you know when I want to know."

Nina nodded. "You do that."

They continued setting the table. Mark was answering some work emails in their bedroom and then would return to the kitchen. Frank had gone to get another chair from the living room to set around the table. He'd stopped haying around 4:30 p.m. and come back to the house to clean up. He said he was going to take the evening off to visit with Paul and Hannah.

That was something new for Abby to hear. Her father didn't usually stop until it was too dark to see. Her dad was slowing down some and taking time off. It was nice to see. Jason must be getting a lot done during the time he was here to help, too. She was happy to see that her parents were managing the farm and doing okay. She knew it was hard work, and she worried about them.

Abby was looking forward to helping in the garden again tomorrow. Since it was Saturday, she anticipated that Mark would be able to help her. He had said he wouldn't work the weekend, which meant he'd check his email occasionally, but otherwise was free.

She smiled. The one thing about her job was if she wasn't at the hospital, there wasn't anything she could do from a distance. It had been great so far this week to be done with work. She couldn't wait until she could do something else, but for now, she was content with letting the situation ride until the adoption plans could be put in motion.

If Madison really wanted to keep her baby, then Abby and Mark could sign up in Houston for places that handled adoptions. She smiled. Why hadn't she thought of adoption sooner? She and Mark had been so set on having their own baby.

Well, she had anyway. Mark must have been thinking about it for a while based on his response when she brought it up. He said he'd been waiting for her to come to the same conclusion. Would she have considered it sooner if he'd brought it up? Maybe not. Maybe she still would have been consumed with the idea of them having their own.

"Abby? Abby?" Nina said.

"What?" She realized she'd been standing in the middle of the kitchen, in the way of her mom and dad, who were trying to set the table and get things out of the oven. Her dad had returned to help while she was standing there pondering the future.

"I asked if you would put butter on the table for the corn and buns."

"Sure." She got the butter out of the fridge and found a bowl to put it in.

"You were thinking hard," her mother said.

"Just about adoption," Abby said, as Mark wandered into the room.

He smiled at her.

Her dad looked over at her. "Your mom told me what happened with Madison today. I'm sorry."

"That's okay, Dad. I saw Madison with little Chloe, and they're meant to be together. Mark and I will find our own little bundle of joy. We'll sign up at adoption agencies when we get back to Houston assuming Madison decides to keep Chloe. It will work out. We just started talking about the process and need to fill out tons of forms. I've heard it can take a while." She smiled at Mark. "We've waited this long. A little longer won't hurt us, but I am anxious to begin the process."

"Me too," Mark said.

They heard a knock on the door, and Abby took a deep breath and let it out. Mark squeezed her hand. "You'll do fine."

They all trooped into the entryway. Mark and Abby stayed back a little way, because there wasn't enough space for all of them. Nina and Frank exchanged hugs with Paul and Hannah. Abby found it interesting that her dad greeted Paul with a hug. It used to be a handshake. Things really had changed.

"Hi, Paul." Abby greeted him but couldn't reach him due to her parents being between them.

"Hello to you two." He smiled at Abby and Mark. "This is my friend Hannah."

They greeted Hannah, and she smiled at them. "It's good to meet you."

Hannah looked right at home with Frank and Nina, and Abby knew she was looking at a future in-law. Abby liked her on sight. She seemed calm and peaceful. Just what Paul needed, Abby realized. Samantha hadn't been calm or peaceful. She'd always been a go-getter.

"Let's move into the kitchen, where there's more room," Nina said.

They all began moving into the kitchen, and Paul asked Frank about the haying. Abby knew Paul had helped Frank with the spring planting and the calving. She also knew Paul had grown up on a farm. His parents had died when he was in college, right before Paul met Samantha. Maybe that was why he took up drinking, although drinking was a usual rite of passage for most teenagers in the state of North Dakota. She briefly thought of her mother telling her to think of another reason Abby might be angry at Paul other than his drinking, but now wasn't the time.

Her mother had directed Paul, Hannah, and Mark to sit at the table. "I think Frank, Abby, and I take up enough room moving around here, so the rest of you just sit and relax."

"Thank you," Hannah said. "We've been sitting and relaxing for the last hour on the drive out here, though, so we would certainly be happy to help."

Nina waved her hand at them. "It's okay. You can help clean up after the meal if you want."

Abby knew that wasn't just to pacify the guests. They'd be helping with dishes if Nina said so.

They soon had everything on the table, said the before-meal prayer, and passed the food around.

"What's happening out here at Chokecherry Valley?" Paul asked. "What are we missing?"

"The Community Helpers group is getting things together for a family who lost everything in a fire. Abby and Mark were out shopping for the family earlier today."

"Oh, we'd like to help too." Paul looked at Hannah. "Do you have plans tomorrow?"

"Nothing that I can't change."

Paul looked back at Nina. "We could help tomorrow, since it's Saturday. I don't work, and Hannah just volunteered."

Hannah laughed at him. "You're lucky I knew why you asked. I'm willing to help, or I would have told you my plans couldn't change."

She looked at Nina. "I'd love to help. What needs to be done yet?"

"Melissa is keeping track of everything. She's the church secretary at St. Anne's Church and the secretary for the Community Helpers group. The Community Helpers group isn't a Catholic group. It's just a bunch of women from around the area who get together, and those who have the time work on various projects."

"That's okay," Hannah said. "I'm glad it's various faiths getting together to work and help others."

"I'll check with Melissa after we eat and see what needs to be done tomorrow. I think right now they're getting the house ready. It needs to be painted and some handyman things done inside to make it livable. It's in pretty good shape, so most things are minor and can be done by anyone."

"Hannah paints. I'm sure she could wield a paintbrush." Paul smiled at her.

"I paint pictures on canvas. Not houses." She laughed. "But sure, if the house needs to be painted, give me a paintbrush, and I'll do boring up-and-down and side-to-side strokes."

They all laughed with her.

Abby decided then that she really liked Hannah. "Well, if they're going to help out, I guess we should volunteer. Right, Mark?"

Mark groaned. "I was waiting for you to say that." Then he grinned. "I'm not going to be outdone by Hannah. If she can pretend to paint, so can I."

Abby looked from her mom to her dad. "Did you have something we need to do around here first before we go over there?"

Nina shooed her away with her hand. "You go help them. Your dad and I will be just fine."

Abby looked at her dad.

"Definitely. Go help them," Frank said.

"Okay."

"Like I said, I'll check with Melissa, and see what she says. I'm guessing there will be quite a number of people there tomorrow working on the project," Nina said.

"We can unload the SUV over there with what we bought today," Abby told Mark.

He just nodded.

Abby was happy Mark was so good-natured. He'd spent the last few months working night and day on his work project, and now during his vacation, she was putting him to work instead of letting him relax. He didn't seem to mind, though.

CHAPTER 15

After they'd finished eating, and everyone helped put away the food and do the dishes, they moved into the living room.

Abby was wondering when she might get Paul alone to apologize, when he asked if she would show him the garden. That made her nervous. When had he ever sought her attention deliberately?

"I helped Nina plant the garden this spring. I need to see how things are growing," he told her as they walked outside.

They took the three steps down from the front door and went around the back of the house where the garden was. It was a gorgeous evening for the last day in June. The birds were chirping. She could hear frogs croaking down by the stream that ran through part of the land.

She twisted her hands together as she stood by the garden. The scent of marigolds and the last of the lilacs perfumed the air.

Paul was walking up and down the rows, inspecting the garden. "Looks pretty good, if I do say so myself." He looked up and smiled at her. "I see you and Nina have gotten some of the weeding done. If I have time this weekend when we're not working at the Community Helpers project, I'll come out here and do some more. I find it relaxing."

Abby gaped at him. "You're so different." She was chagrined at her words but could only stand there stunned.

He stood where he was in the middle of the garden. "I hope so, Abby. I'm sorry for the way I behaved. Before and after Sam's death. I loved her, and I know you did too. We both lost someone precious to us when she died. I understand why you yelled at me at the cemetery. I deserved it. While Sam chose to drink, I didn't do much to dissuade her. I yelled at her a lot, which didn't do a lot of good. I should have taken Amy away from her, and maybe at least Amy would be alive. But I didn't. She loved Amy so much, I could never have taken her away from her mother." He cleared his throat. "Now they're both gone. In heaven is my belief."

Abby couldn't think of anything to say, and then the words came. "It's not your fault, Paul. I know that I blamed you at the cemetery that day, but it was my grief lashing out at you. I blamed you for many years for my sister's drinking, but the truth is more complicated than that. You drank, but then you stopped. First, I blamed you for drinking with her, and then I blamed you when you didn't force her to stop drinking after you stopped. The truth is, Sam chose to drink. The disease of alcoholism had her wrapped around in circles, and she couldn't get out. I don't know why she didn't try. Or maybe she did try, but she never told us because it didn't work."

"She loved Amy," said Paul. "If she could have done it for anybody, she would have done it for her, but she didn't. Sometimes, people just don't know the right steps to take. That's the way it was for her."

They stood silently for a few minutes, and Abby realized something else. She knew what her mother was talking about when she said that the drinking wasn't the only reason Abby was angry at Paul. "I felt you took her away from me. That's the other reason I was angry. I blamed you that she never came to Houston to visit. I know it wasn't your fault. Sam made her own decisions."

"If it helps you to know, I suggested many times we should visit you in Houston, but she said no. She felt like you had your life together and she didn't."

Abby laughed bitterly at that. "I should have come out here and talked some sense into her. She had some of what I wanted, and I had some of what she wanted. I wasted time being angry at her too. I guess I just pretended it was only you I was mad at, but the truth is, I was jealous of both of you.

"I felt you took my sister away. And then she got pregnant easily and had a baby. I wanted a child so bad, and she had no problem, and then drank her life away."

"Are you still angry at me, Abby? Because if you are, I'll make some excuse for tomorrow, so we aren't working in the same area of the house. Or I can come a different day when you're not there."

Abby thought about it. She realized that by talking to Paul, a lot of her angry feelings toward him were gone. So was the jealousy that had been eating away at her. She felt calmer over what had happened. Now, she mostly felt sadness in the pit of her stomach. She'd always miss Sam and Amy.

She took a few steps toward Paul. "We can all work together tomorrow. I'm not mad any longer. You did the best you could. I miss them both, but I'm sure you do too."

"I miss them every day, but I'm lucky to have Hannah now."

"How about a hug to seal the deal?" she asked.

Paul held out his arms, and she took the few remaining steps to his side. His hug was warm and comforting. "Thank you," he said. "I really want us to be friends."

She stepped away and smiled at him. "I believe we are," she said softly. "I hope for the best with you and Hannah. You deserve happiness, Paul. Thank you for bringing me out to the garden tonight, so we could talk this through."

"You're welcome. I'm happy too. I hope you and Mark have a child. You would make a great mother." He started walking down the row out of the garden, and she followed.

CHAPTER 16

The next day, Frank headed out to the field. Jason wasn't coming over because he had agreed to do some of the plumbing repairs at the Meyer family house.

Abby and Mark drove over to the Meyers' house-in-progress in their SUV, and Nina drove separately. Their vehicles were both loaded with new items for the family along with cleaning supplies and other things Melissa had requested. Nina had found a few outside decorations that she and Hannah had discussed the night before, and Hannah had said she could repaint the garden gnomes, turtles, and some other things for the Meyers so they would have some decorations in their front yard.

Nina had talked to Melissa the night before as planned, and Melissa had told them she'd hand out assignments when they arrived.

As Abby got out of the SUV she looked around at the flurry of activity. There were at least ten people already working on the outside, and she wondered how many were inside. There were cars and pickups lined up along the roadside, and Mark had parked along the road too. They left all their things in the vehicle until they knew what Melissa had planned.

Melissa stood at the door to the house. It was propped open so that people could come and go easily. She directed Abby into the house, through the kitchen, and into the living room. "How about you join Hannah and Christina in painting the living room," she suggested to Abby and Nina. "They got here just a little bit ago and are just starting."

Hannah and Christina said hello, and Brooke came running up to Abby. "Will you help us?"

Abby squatted down and gave the little girl a hug. "Of course. We're going to paint. What are you going to do?"

"I get to paint too." She pointed to a little can of paint that was open, and a little mini brush. "It's just my size."

Abby's heart swelled with love for the little girl. "It sure is. You'll do a great job."

She stood up and looked back at Mark. "I guess I'm painting. Do you want to check with Melissa about your job?"

Mark shrugged. "She already told me I'm in the back with some other guys clearing out the backyard. It's full of dead things and leaves and branches." He shuddered, and then broke into a big grin. "What fun. I can't look at my computer all day." He left.

She laughed. "He's been looking for a break from that laptop for weeks. This will be good for him, but he's going to be sore at the end of the day."

Christina laughed with her. "We're all going to be sore at the end of the day."

They started taping so the window frames wouldn't get paint on them, and then continued taping around other borders. Hannah took the light-switch covers off with a screwdriver and grunted every once in a while when she came to a screw that refused to budge.

"Why don't you leave those really hard ones, and we'll get one of the guys to take them off. They can do it in a second. It will save you some energy," Abby said.

"Then I'd have to admit I'm a poor, weak woman," Hannah argued.

"No, you won't. We'll grab one of those guys doing the electricity or plumbing. They don't know us. Mark and Paul are in the backyard, and they'll never know."

"That's true," Hannah grinned. "You've sold me on the idea."

The women worked companionably and joked and laughed. Brooke floated from person to person, interrupting with some innocent question and then going back to drawing pictures on her corner of the wall. Some of the volunteers brought them sandwiches and bottles of water for lunch, and the men took a break and joined them in the bare living room.

"Wow, you've made progress," Mark said when he came in.

Everything they didn't want painted had the edges taped, and the switch plates had all been removed. They had started painting one of the walls a creamy beige. Abby had started on one side, and Nina had started on the other.

Hannah had said she'd paint up by the ceiling, so she had climbed the ladder by the opposite wall and painted a section while Christina stayed by the ladder and made sure it was stable.

Then they'd move it a little more. It was slow going, but they had a start.

Lunch was brief, and they all started back in on their assigned tasks. The women in the living room wanted to get the room painted before the end of the day. The men had decided they wanted to get the backyard cleaned before they left, so they were all in a hurry to continue.

When the day was done, the volunteer teams had most of the house painted and most of the exterior cleaned up. Melissa thought they might be able to get the outside of the house painted and the rest of the landscaping done the next weekend. They were lucky the roof didn't need to be redone.

Some of the volunteers said they could come in Monday and finish up the inside painting. The flooring was getting installed on Wednesday, the day after the Fourth of July, so nothing could be done inside on that day. And nobody planned to work on the Fourth of July as there was a parade in a neighboring town, and a lot of people had company and fireworks planned for that day. They were lucky the year had been wet enough that they could shoot off fireworks in the county.

CHAPTER 17

Abby went to church at St. Anne's with her parents on Sunday morning. After supper Thursday evening, Nina had already invited Paul and Hannah to join them at the house after church. At church, she invited Christina and Brooke to also join them. They all met for brunch.

Paul and Hannah had brought an assortment of blueberry, raspberry, and banana muffins. They'd also brought all the ingredients and insisted they were cooking the omelets and hash browns for the brunch. Abby tried to join them in the kitchen, but she was sent back to the living room to talk with Christina and play with Brooke.

In the living room, Mark sat talking to Frank, while Abby played on the floor with Brooke and her toy cars. Abby listened in to the conversation her mom was having with Christina.

It was a pleasant morning, and Abby knew she was going to miss the whole bunch of them when she returned to Houston. Her home was going to be very quiet compared to her parents' constant activity. She and Mark had let work become their whole way of life. Either she was on shift at the hospital or Mark was working on his computer. They hadn't connected in a long time. She realized that situation needed to change.

There was no reason for her not to have talked to Mark about her quitting her job. The fact that she hadn't told Mark yet indicated a fault in their marriage that needed to be corrected, especially if they were going to raise a child together. She wasn't sure why she feared him knowing about her leaving her job. Maybe she thought he would try to convince her to continue working there even though she was so unhappy. She didn't know. The sooner she talked about it with him, the sooner it would be clear in her head.

Mark might appreciate that she was considering a different job. Maybe she'd get a job at a clinic working for a physician. She'd only be working weekdays, because most clinics were closed on the weekend. She smiled at the thought.

"Can I play on the piano?" Brooke pointed to the piano that was along one wall in the living room.

"It's kind of noisy," Abby told her, thinking of everybody else in the room talking.

"That's okay," Nina told her. She must have overheard Brooke's request. "We won't be disturbed."

Abby knew her mom missed hearing Sam play. Sam had been the musician in the family. Abby had given up learning the piano. She just didn't have the patience for it.

She helped Brooke get up on the piano stool, and then she opened the lid. Brooke made lots of noise, and the adults in the room indulgently listened to her pound away. After about five minutes, the newness wore off, and Brooke quit. Abby closed the piano lid.

Instead of getting down, Brooke wanted to look at the pictures on the top of the piano. Abby went and sat in a wing chair across from the couch where her mom and Christina were sitting. Brooke had then climbed down from the piano bench and leaned against the chair's arm where Abby sat. The women were all having a conversation when Brooke interrupted.

"I talked to that girl," she said.

Abby looked down at her. "What girl?"

"The one in the picture on the piano."

Abby got up and followed Brooke back over to the piano. There were some pictures of her and Sam when they were small, and there were a few pictures of Amy sitting at the piano. "Which little girl?"

Brooke pointed to one of the pictures of Amy. "That little girl. She told me I'm going to get a new mommy and daddy."

Christina gasped. "When did she tell you that?" She got up from the couch and hurried over to Brooke. She scrunched on her haunches looking at her.

"When we were at Madison's house looking at the baby."

The adults looked at each other wide-eyed.

"I don't think that's true, Brooke. That little girl wasn't at Madison's house. You know what I said about telling stories," Christina said. She looked at the others. "Brooke has a vivid imagination."

"It's okay," Nina said, though her voice was tight, and her face was white. "We understand."

Brooke looked at Christina uncertainly. "Did I do something wrong?"

"No, honey. Of course not. You just go ahead and play now. I need to talk to Nina."

Mark came to the rescue. "I can take her outside if you want. She can play until brunch is ready," he said to Christina.

"Let's go outside, Brooke," he said to her. "I'm sure there must be something interesting growing in the garden."

"Yay! I get to go outside." Brooke skipped out of the room, and Mark followed.

A moment of silence descended on the room once she was gone. Then Christina collapsed on the couch and leaned back. "Wow. I'm so sorry she brought up Amy. I'm sure it must be hard to hear about her. Brooke didn't really understand what she was saying."

"It's okay," Nina said. She hesitated for a moment. "Can I tell you a family secret, Christina? This needs to stay between us."

Christina straightened up on the couch and took a deep breath. "Of course, I'll keep whatever you have to say a secret. I don't usually go blabbing things to others."

Nina patted her hand. "I didn't mean to hurt your feelings, but this is kind of different and might be hard to understand. It involves Paul, and I think he should be the one to tell you. I'm just going to go talk to him for a minute."

She left the room to talk to Paul.

Abby sat there wondering what it was that Paul had to do with Brooke's pretend game of talking to Amy. Little kids always had imaginary friends, and Brooke just saw the picture and wanted to pretend she and Amy had talked. It really sounded as if Brooke wanted to be part of a family with a mother and father. The picture she had pointed at was a family picture of Sam, Paul, and Amy.

Nina came back into the room, with Paul and Hannah behind her. They were smiling, so obviously Paul wasn't upset by what Nina told them. Abby noticed Paul and Hannah were holding hands. Hannah must be a great support to Paul, based on his reaction.

Paul went directly over to Christina, and he and Hannah settled on the couch beside her. "I hope you're okay, Christina. That must have been a shock to hear Brooke mention a mom and dad."

"It was. You see, her parents divorced and neither wants her. They left her with me two years ago and haven't once been back to see her. They're just traveling and seeing the world and each doing their own thing. Neither one has barely asked about her at all. I hardly know where they are. Once in a while, one of them might call and that's it. I'm considering adopting her myself or seeing if there's a couple who would be interested in adopting her. When I heard her say she would have a new mom and dad…well…it almost seemed like someone else would be adopting her. But I know she couldn't have talked to Amy. It's all confusing."

"We'll get to Amy in a minute, but I do want to know if you really want to adopt Brooke. If you do, I think you should get it done and sealed before either of her parents change their mind. Obviously, they're not fit parents if they really don't want Brooke. She deserves better than that."

"I've put it off, thinking they'll be back." She looked down at her hands, twisting them in her lap. "I have to admit my daughter and son-in-law just don't care. That's hard, because Brooke is such a sweet little girl. I will move forward with adoption after the Fourth of July. You're right, I shouldn't put it off. Physically my arthritis is starting to act up, and I wish her to have two parents, but I don't know how to go about finding someone who would love her as much as I do. I should just go forward and adopt her. I know she wants a dad, but I guess that's something I can't give her."

Paul squeezed her hands and let go. "It might work out yet. You never know, but we'll leave that for a few days. Let's talk about what she said about Amy." He looked around the room. "It might be true that she talked to Amy."

Abby felt the room spin and then right itself. Her mom and dad didn't look surprised, she noticed. Christina looked puzzled.

"I saw Amy myself right after she died," Paul said. "I know it's hard to believe, but whenever I was in extreme distress, she would come and talk to me. Although I was shocked when she appeared, her presence was always a great source of comfort for me. I believe God sent her from Heaven to comfort me."

Abby had thought he was calm about sharing the information until she saw how tightly he was now holding Hannah's hand.

"I haven't seen her for quite a while. I guess she had someone else she needed to comfort. Brooke." He paused and looked at Christina. "I don't know if you'll believe me, but Amy probably did talk to Brooke. As far as what that means when she told her she'd have a new mommy and daddy, I don't know. I saw Amy several times after her death. Seeing her, and knowing she was okay, helped me get through these months since her and Samantha's deaths. I'm sure you'll need to think about what I've said, and what you believe, but that was my experience."

Paul looked at Abby. "I was going to tell you the other night when I was here, but we got sidetracked. You know now." Paul stood up and looked at Christina. "Let me know if you have questions, but as Nina said, I'd appreciate this conversation be kept confidential for obvious reasons. Other people probably won't understand."

"Brunch will be ready in about ten minutes. I'll let you finish your conversation, and then you can join us in the kitchen whenever you're ready," Paul said before returning to the kitchen.

There was silence when he was gone.

Finally, Christina broke the silence that had settled when Paul and Hannah left the room. "I don't know what to think."

Frank and Nina looked at each other and then both laughed. Nina said, "We don't either. Paul told us this summer what he experienced. We find it hard to believe, but whatever happened, it helped him. He'll never get over missing Amy, nor will we. But it helped him to know she seems okay, and she says she's in heaven. We believe that, so we just accept it. You do what you have to do, Christina. Just know Frank and I will help you however we can with Brooke. If you decide to adopt her officially, we'll definitely help you in whatever way we can."

Abby didn't know what to think. Paul really seemed to believe what he said, and he was normally very pragmatic. She couldn't believe he'd been having conversations with Amy. She was also stunned by the realization of what Brooke's parents had done. They'd just left their little girl. From what Christina said, they didn't seem to want Brooke. How could they not want that sweet little girl?

The rest of the visit proceeded with lots of laughter. Since Hannah and Paul had made the brunch, Mark and Abby cleaned up. Christina had taken Brooke home right after they finished eating, so she could have her nap. The rest of them played cards until late afternoon, and then Paul and Hannah went back to Bismarck.

CHAPTER 18

Abby waited impatiently for the evening meal to be over. She'd been thinking about Brooke and wanted to talk to Mark, but there was the meal to get ready and the outside chores to be done.

Sunday was generally quiet around the farm, but there were still chickens, cows, and calves to be fed. Mark had gone with her dad to take care of them, and she and her mom straightened out the house. They were going back to the Meyers' house tomorrow to help with whatever they could.

Finally, Abby suggested a walk with Mark so they could talk. Her parents were settled in front of the television and were quite happy to relax, she could tell.

Abby applied bug spray and handed the bottle to Mark as they stood on the porch of the house. "Let's stick to the road. Hopefully, there will be fewer bugs."

"Sounds good," Mark said, after he'd sprayed himself and followed her down the steps. "This might be a short walk, if they're as bad as I think they're going to be."

Abby agreed. She could hear the buzzing of insects as they walked down the driveway.

"I know what you're going to say," Mark said as they walked. "You want to talk about Brooke."

"You're right. How could her parents just dump her on Christina and not check on her? I don't understand how anyone can do that."

"Not everyone is cut out to be a parent."

Abby stopped short and stared at him. "Are you saying it's okay that they just abandoned her?"

He put up his hands to placate her. "No. That's not what I meant at all. I'm agreeing with you. They obviously don't want to be parents. They haven't grown up, and Christina's doing a marvelous job with Brooke. She's a sweet little girl."

Abby relaxed her shoulders. "She is, isn't she? That was nice of you to take her outside while we talked. Dad filled you in on what Paul said, didn't he?"

"Yes. He took me aside while the rest of you were busy."

"I kind of thought so, since you weren't surprised when I said Brooke's parents had abandoned her."

Abby couldn't hold back her eagerness any longer. "What if we adopted her, Mark? Her parents don't want her. Christina isn't sure she can take care of her by herself, though she will if there's no other good choice for Brooke."

Mark didn't say anything right away. She could tell he was thinking about it. "I just don't know, Abby. When we talked about adopting, we were thinking of a baby. I know we mentioned in passing an older child, but now that that might be a possibility, I see lots of problems."

Abby was disappointed that he wasn't as excited as her. "I just feel like it might be a sign, since we're here when Brooke said she saw Amy, and Amy mentioned Brooke getting a new mommy and daddy."

"Do you really believe she saw Amy?"

Abby shrugged. "I don't know. I don't think it matters."

"You love Amy. What do you mean, you don't think it matters?"

"I think what matters is what Brooke thinks. She believes she's going to get a new family. We could be that family."

"What about Brooke seeing her grandmother? We rarely see your parents. We'd be taking her back to Houston with us. She wouldn't get to see Christina very often.

Abby hadn't considered that. "We could move back to Chokecherry Valley," she said impulsively.

Mark swatted at a mosquito on his sleeve, and then reached toward Abby as they stood in the driveway. "As much as we need to talk about this, I don't think this is the place. There are too many bugs out here tonight." He brushed a fly off her arm. "We're going to get eaten alive. Let's wait until we get back inside."

"Do we keep this to ourselves or mention it to mom and dad?" she asked, disappointed that Mark hadn't immediately jumped on the idea of adopting Brooke. She realized that she had felt the urge to adopt Chloe only a few days ago. Maybe it was time to slow down and think instead of rushing forward.

"You can talk to them about us wanting to adopt, but I think we should tell them not to mention anything to Christina or Madison. I really don't want to talk with anyone else about it until we talk about it more ourselves and decide what we want to do."

"That's fine with me," Abby said. A little more time was just what they needed. Madison and Christina each needed to decide what they wanted to do.

Mark reached out and drew her to him in a hug. "I know what you want, honey. A bigger family. I do too. I just think we need to really think about this and do the right thing. We just found out this morning that Brooke might need a new family, although Christina will do a wonderful job alone. I'm not worried about Brooke. We just need to consider what would happen if we did decide to adopt. Is that the right thing for Brooke? And us? We need to think about it."

Abby snuggled up to him. He smelled of fabric softener and bug spray. "You're right. I need to curb my impatience and make the right decision for all of us."

"It's one of your lovable qualities. I love your enthusiasm."

She looked up at him, and he kissed her on the lips. "And I love you," she said.

"Ditto."

#

When they got back to their room later, Abby realized Mark hadn't said anything in response to her suggestion that they move back to Chokecherry Valley. She wasn't sure if he'd purposely avoided the topic or if the adoption discussion had taken precedence.

They were getting ready for bed, but Abby planned to read for a while, and Mark planned to look at work emails. Abby waited until Mark had closed the laptop and put it on the floor beside the bed. She'd sporadically flipped pages of her book, not actually reading a thing, while he'd read his emails. She placed the bookmark where she had stopped reading earlier and closed the book.

"How about a game of rummy?" Mark asked. "It's too early for bed."

Abby scooted up to sit straighter against the headboard. "I was going to talk to you about something."

Mark walked over and sat against the headboard next to her. "What about?"

She didn't blame him for the note of uncertainty in his voice. A lot had happened since she had come to Chokecherry Valley. Or a lot of things that had lain dormant had come to the surface. "It's about the comment I made earlier about moving to Chokecherry Valley."

Mark looked at her, his forehead crinkled in concentration. "I thought you just said that because you wanted to adopt Brooke. I didn't realize you were serious."

Abby looked down at her pajama bottoms and folded part of the material between her fingers before smoothing it out again. "I don't know about the moving to Chokecherry Valley part. I quit my job in Houston. It isn't the right place for me anymore."

"You quit? When?" he asked quietly.

She looked at him and could tell he was upset by his clenched hands. "The day before I left Houston."

"And you are just telling me now? We have a big problem, Abby, and a baby isn't going to fix that problem."

"What do you mean by that?" The sadness in his eyes tugged at her heart. He didn't seem angry. He seemed hurt, which she had expected when she first started keeping the secret.

"We don't talk anymore about things, and we need to do that. I don't care that you quit your job if you were unhappy with it. I care that we didn't discuss it either before you quit or right after."

Abby knew she should have said something sooner. "I agree we don't talk enough. I'm tired of shift work. I'd like to go to work and come home at basically the same time every day. With you working on IT projects, there are some weeks that we rarely see each other. I don't want us turning into strangers."

Mark reached over and pulled her close to his side and kept his arm around her. She laid her head on his shoulder. "I don't want us turning into strangers either. We need to communicate with each other, though, or we won't have a marriage. Have you looked at other jobs yet?"

"No. We've been kind of busy, and I've just been thinking about it a lot. I guess I wanted to hear what you had to say before I started looking."

"Right." He laughed.

"What does that mean?" She looked up at him.

"It means as soon as you had a little energy back, you would have looked no matter what I said." He hugged her close. "Which you know would be all right with me."

She laughed too and snuggled back beside him. "You're right. I'm glad you agree, but I would have started looking for a different job. In Houston."

"In Houston. But now we're here in Chokecherry Valley, and we might adopt a child from here. And so, you're now thinking about maybe moving here?"

He said it as a question.

"Yes. If we were able to adopt either Madison's baby or Brooke, it would be hard to separate them from their loved ones. But it's also a huge step to move from Houston to Chokecherry Valley. I think I'd rather move to Bismarck if we move to North Dakota. It's a bigger place, and I wouldn't have any trouble finding a job. And if the adoption originated in Chokecherry Valley and we lived in Bismarck, we'd still be close enough for visits."

"No, you wouldn't have trouble finding work. I think we could move anywhere, and there would be a nursing job available."

"I think so too."

"I don't think we can make a decision about moving until the situation with Madison's baby or Brooke is sorted out. If we did adopt one of those children, we'd have to think seriously about what to do. Right now, it's just kind of a 'what if' scenario."

"I know." Abby was content that Mark hadn't seemed upset by the conversation. He hadn't said no right away, which was a good sign. "I think you could find a job or telecommute to Houston if you wanted."

"I agree. But of course, I haven't looked or thought about it until today." He laughed, looking down at her. "You keep my life interesting, Abby. I don't know what I'd do without you."

"Your life would be simpler," she replied.

"But boring. Very boring looking at the computer all day long."

"That's right."

He took her by the shoulders and looked into her eyes. "You need to tell me what's going on, Abby. Whether you want to adopt a child or get a different job, we need to communicate with each other. Agreed?"

"Agreed." She knew she needed to be more open with him. Samantha's death had caused her to close herself off, and she needed to get past that to keep her marriage strong.

CHAPTER 19

Monday passed quickly as the volunteers put the final touches on the Meyers' new farmhouse. Abby and Mark unloaded their SUV of the things they'd bought the previous week and made another trip to Bismarck for a few more necessities.

Tuesday morning, Abby woke up excited for the Fourth of July celebration. She always liked fireworks, but she was also looking forward to the picnic after the parade. A lot of her graduating class would attend the picnic, and she wanted to catch up with them.

There was also the additional excitement of seeing Madison and Chloe and finding out if Madison had made a final decision about adoption. She was sure Madison would have spoken to her mother by now about wanting to keep the baby, but there was still a chance she would give the baby up. Abby had wanted to quiz Jason when he came over for haying, but she'd left him alone. It wouldn't be fair to put him on the spot.

At the community Fourth of July picnic, Abby and Mark went through the food line. Her parents had already gotten their own food and joined some friends of theirs at a table.

Abby was trying to decide between potato salad and coleslaw when she realized Madison and Patricia were seated with Brooke and Christina, and there was room at their picnic table for Mark and her. She thrust her plate at Mark.

"Can you get me some potato salad and a hamburger with ketchup?" she asked. "I'm going to save us a seat over there." She pointed to the group she wanted to join.

Mark agreed, and she took off to join the others. "Hi," she greeted them all.

They looked up from their plates and smiled.

"Do you want to sit with us?" Christina asked.

"We'd love to. Mark's getting some food for me. He should be here soon." She gestured toward the food-laden tables.

"It's good," Madison said shyly.

"I see you're without Chloe today. Is she home with a babysitter?" Abby asked.

"Jason had some time off and wanted to watch her. He said he doesn't get enough time to spend with his niece since he's always working, and this would be a good opportunity. I felt funny leaving her, as I haven't done that before, but I keep my phone handy."

Abby noticed the pink-encased phone sitting on the table near Madison. "I'm sure Jason is a fine babysitter. I know he's a lot older than you because he was in school with my brother-in-law, who is twenty-nine."

"Yes, he is older and a good uncle," Patricia agreed. "We'll only be here for a short time and then be back home." She patted Madison on the back.

Abby knew she couldn't ask Madison her plans in front of everyone. She bit back a sigh and greeted Mark enthusiastically when he brought her plate of food and set it in front of her. "Thank you," she said.

He smiled and sat down beside her. "Hi. It's great to see all of you again," he said to the group as he scooped up some of the coleslaw on his plate.

They all greeted him, and there was happy silence as they all continued eating.

Brooke had been intently coloring during the greetings, but now she slid off the picnic table bench and brought her picture over to Abby. She held it up for inspection. "Look what I drew."

Abby put her fork down and took the picture from Brooke. "It's lovely. Do you want to tell me about it?"

Brooke shifted back and forth from one foot to the other as she pointed out different colors on the paper. "That's a tree, and some flowers, and that's grass."

"It's lovely," Abby told her, reaching to hand the picture back to Brooke.

"You can keep it," Brooke said. "I'll make another one for Grandma."

"Thank you." Abby was touched by the gesture. "I'll put this one up on my wall."

Brooke skipped back to her place at the table and started another picture.

Mark patted Abby on the shoulder. "She really likes you," he whispered.

Abby smiled at him. "I like her too."

They all had a pleasant conversation, and then Madison got up to leave. "I really need to get back to Chloe and give Jason some time to do whatever he wants."

Abby stood up. She felt this might be her chance to talk to Madison alone. "Do you mind if we talk for a minute?"

Madison looked at her mom.

Patricia smiled and waved with her hand. "I'll meet you at the pickup in a little bit."

Abby waited until they were in the parking lot before she said anything. When Madison stopped by a blue pickup, she looked at Abby. "Thank you for talking to me the other day when I was so upset. I really needed to talk, and you were so kind."

Abby smiled at her, though she was trembling inside with nerves. "You're welcome. Did you talk to your mom and make a decision?"

"I did talk to Mom. It really helped." Madison wore a big smile now. "I'm going to keep Chloe, and Mom said she would help. She was really supportive. She said we would make it work out somehow."

Abby hid her disappointment. She knew this could happen, but she still had hopes that maybe Chloe would be the baby for her and Mark. That wasn't possible any longer. "That's good, Madison. I'm glad it all worked out."

She heard someone approaching and looked to see Patricia coming their way. "There's your mom."

"Did you get to talk?" Patricia asked them.

"Yes," Abby said. "Thank you. If you have time, why don't you all come over to the house before I leave for Houston next Tuesday. Mom would love to chat with you," she said to Patricia.

"We'd enjoy that. With taking care of Chloe and trying to get the Meyer house completed, we haven't had much down time to visit, but we'll make time," Patricia said.

"That sounds good. See you soon." Abby stepped out of the way and stood in the parking lot after they'd driven away. Their decision had saddened her, and it made her realize that much more how deeply she wanted a baby of her own. She needed to have patience. She and Mark had just started looking, and they wouldn't find a baby overnight. She went back to join the others and tried to enjoy the rest of the day with her family.

CHAPTER 20

That evening Abby and Mark sat on some folding chairs they had brought to the fireworks display. The fireworks were being set off in a clearing near the town, and the whole town had gathered around with chairs and blankets to sit on and watch the display. Abby's parents had joined them, and the four of them sat chatting and enjoying the warm night as they waited for the display to start.

Abby looked at the group of people around them and smiled. In the week she'd been back to Chokecherry Valley, she'd reconnected with old friends and made new ones. She felt lucky.

She snuggled her chair closer to Mark and took his hand. He patted it, and then held it firmly in his. She treasured the feeling of closeness. They had talked more and gotten closer during this trip, and she knew that would help their relationship long-term and when they found the right baby to adopt.

She noticed Christina and Brooke, and they were looking her way, so she waved at them. She caught a glimpse of a woman behind them and squeezed Mark's hand tightly.

"Look behind Christina and Brooke," she whispered.

He turned his head toward them and waved because they were still looking toward their direction.

"Behind them," Abby gasped. "That woman looks like Samantha."

Mark turned further and looked around. "I don't see anyone behind them that looks like her. I just see a bunch of teenage boys."

Abby stared at the area behind Christina and Brooke. She saw the boys too, but she also saw the woman. The woman was pointing at Brooke. And then she disappeared. Abby jumped up from her chair. She needed to find that woman. She hurried through the groups of people to Christina and Brooke and looked around, but the woman was gone. Her heart was beating fast, and she was near tears.

Mark was just behind her, and she turned around and fell into his arms. "It looked just like her. She was pointing at Brooke."

He held her close. "Do you want to stay and watch the fireworks, or should we leave?"

"I want to leave." She felt close to tears and didn't want to break down in front of everyone. She missed Samantha, even though they'd had their differences.

She felt a tug on her short pants and looked down to see Brooke standing there, grinning widely up at her.

"Hi," Brooke said. "We're waiting to watch the fireworks. Do you want to sit with me?"

Abby pulled herself together enough to answer. "We're already sitting over there with my parents." She pointed over to them. They were both staring at her and Mark, probably wondering why they had suddenly left.

Brooke patted her hand. "They can come over here too."

Abby smiled down at her and looked around. "There really isn't room here. There are already lots of people. We'll go back to our chairs and talk to you after the fireworks."

She and Mark and her parents had set their chairs a little further away at the edge of the crowd. Abby was glad for that now. She just wanted to sit down and have Mark hold her hand again.

Brooke had turned to talk to Christina, and soon she was back. "Grandma said we can sit over there with you since there's more room."

Abby looked at Mark, and he shrugged, leaving it up to her. Abby dredged up a smile. "Sure. We'll help you move your things."

Soon Christina and Brooke were settled beside Abby and Mark. Her parents accepted the change in company with a smile.

When the fireworks started, there were lots of oohing and aahing from the spectators. Brooke jumped up and down with excitement. The noise didn't seem to bother her, and she kept commenting on how high the fireworks shot into the sky.

Abby found herself enjoying the show in spite of her spinning thoughts. She knew there was no way Samantha had been in the crowd, but the woman had looked so much like her, and then she'd just disappeared. Abby shivered, and Mark noticed.

"Are you cold? Do we need to pull out a sweater?"

Abby looked at the others to make sure they weren't listening. Everyone was distracted by the fireworks. "No. I was just thinking about that woman."

"You know it couldn't be your sister, right?" Mark looked worried.

"I know. It was just so strange. And she pointed right at Brooke."

Brooke, hearing her name, looked up at them from her place on the blanket where she was now sitting. She'd worn herself out. "Will you be my mommy and daddy?" she asked.

Christina instantly took Brooke's hand and frowned at her. "Honey. Why did you ask them that?"

Brooke pulled her hand away. "A lady told me tonight that I was getting a new mommy and daddy, and I like Abby and him." She looked shyly at Mark.

It was the first time Abby had seen her acting shy since she met Brooke at the church that first morning.

Christina shrugged helplessly as an awkward silence fell on the group.

Mark broke the silence. "Let's talk about that tomorrow morning, okay." He leaned down and patted Brooke's hand. "It's late, and we all need to get some sleep."

Abby was glad for the respite. She needed to get away from all these people. She stood and folded her chair. "It looks like the fireworks are over. I'm tired."

Soon they were all gathering their things and saying goodnight. Abby saw Mark speak to

Christina for a few minutes, but she didn't hear
what he said. She was too tired and strung out to
care. She just wanted to get back to her parents'
house and calm down.

CHAPTER 21

Abby had showered and hurried into her pajamas. She now sat with her back against the headboard in their bedroom at her parents' house. Mark was taking his shower, and she was glad to be alone for a few minutes.

Had she seen her sister at the fireworks? Or had it just been her imagination? The picture was so vivid. And the woman had pointed right at Brooke. And then Brooke had asked her and Mark to be her parents. What did it mean?

Mark came out of the bathroom in his pajama bottoms and joined her. He leaned against the headboard and pulled her to him, and she relaxed against him.

"Quite a night," he said.

"That's for sure." She snuggled closer.

He took in a big breath and let it go. She looked up at him. "Are you feeling tense?"

He leaned down and kissed her forehead. "I have a confession to make."

She could feel him tense up again and sat up. She felt she was going to need to have this conversation face-to-face.

"I saw her," Mark said.

"Saw who?"

"The woman you saw. She looked just like Samantha. Just like you said. And I saw her point at Brooke." He dropped his gaze and then looked at her again. "I'm sorry I said I didn't see her. I was afraid."

"Afraid?"

"Remember when Brooke told us she spoke to a little girl, and that girl looked like Amy? And she said she was getting a new mommy and daddy. It was hard to believe. Kids have imaginary friends all the time. But then tonight…" He shrugged. "The woman was pointing at Brooke, and I knew what that meant, and I was afraid I couldn't do it."

Abby's stomach was flipping at what her husband was saying. He'd seen the woman too. She was beginning to think it really was her sister, Samantha. Samantha coming to her to let her know that Abby would be Brooke's new mother. She felt a moment of joy at the thought, but she and Mark had to sort this out. "Afraid you couldn't do what?"

"Raise a child. What if I'm not very good at it? Everything keeps pointing at Brooke being the child for us to adopt. I thought we'd adopt a baby and learn together. Brooke already has a grandmother, and a mother who doesn't want her. She's already learned so much, and we're coming into her life in the middle of things."

Abby reached out and hugged Mark. "She already loves us, Mark. That's the biggest hurdle. She wants a mom and dad, and she wants us."

She took his hand and squeezed it. "Do you want to adopt her? Don't say it just for me. Say if for yourself and for Brooke too. Only if you want to."

He smiled. A smile that took over his whole face. "I really want to adopt her. For me, and for you—and for her. I love her already. She's the sweetest little girl."

CHAPTER 22

September had come to Chokecherry Valley, and it was a warm fall day. Leaves were starting to turn bright yellow and red and orange.

Abby and Mark had moved to Bismarck in August, but today was a special day. They were at Frank and Nina's house spreading balloons throughout the living room. Abby had baked a chocolate cake with chocolate frosting because that was what Brooke had requested. There was only one candle on the cake, and writing that said, "Welcome Home." Beside the cake, a glass unicorn from Abby's parents and a stuffed elephant from Mark and Abby sat on the table with two cards. Abby was getting nervous.

"I hope she likes it," Abby said to her mom.

Her mom gave her a big hug. "She loves you and Mark. I bet she doesn't stop talking from the moment she runs in the front door."

Mark and Frank joined them in the kitchen.

"We're ready," Mark gave Abby a big grin. He had come to terms with adopting Brooke and his fear of not being a perfect dad. Love was all that mattered.

The four of them looked at each other as they heard the sound of an engine coming up the driveway. Christina and Brooke had arrived.

"Show time," Frank said.

They all laughed nervously as they went to the front door to greet their new family.

Abby opened the door, and Brooke came running in. She headed straight for Mark. "Are you my new daddy?" she asked.

He picked her up in his arms and smiled at her. "Today's the day. The paperwork is official. I'm your dad."

He reached out his hand to Abby and drew her into the circle of his embrace. "And Abby is your new mom."

Brooke leaned toward Abby and put her little hands on Abby's cheeks. "I love you, Mommy," she said.

"I love you too, Brooke," Abby choked out her response and held back her happy tears as she kissed Brooke on the cheek. She had a child and a husband and a new job in Bismarck.

In the background, unseen by the others in the room, stood Samantha. Happy tears streamed down her face as she watched her twin sister get the child she had always wanted. Samantha knew that Abby had been jealous of her pregnancy and Amy's birth, yet had also been heartbroken at their deaths.

The addition of Brooke to Abby's family would help heal the wound of being unable to have her own children. And Abby and Mark would help heal Brooke's wound of being abandoned. Brooke would bring so much love to their family, all with God's blessing.

~ ~ ~

Read the next Chokecherry Valley book.

Picture of Book 3
Chokecherry Valley Love

Ashley Richmond's lifelong dream to become a psychologist suddenly seems to be the wrong path for her. She meets an intriguing young man in one of her classes, which adds an additional complication to her decisions.

After being estranged from her family for two years, she decides it's time to put the past behind her and begin repairing her relationships with them.

COPYRIGHT

ABOUT THE AUTHOR

Jean Rezab writes from her home in North Dakota. She loves the wide-open prairie and spring wildflowers. She's an avid mystery reader.